More praise from the cast of *Beverly Hills, 90210*

In the world of teen drama, I can't imagine a
more entertaining writer than Larry Mollin.

—Brian Austin Green

The writer Larry Mollin was entrusted
with Donna losing her virginity!
What more is there to say?

—Tori Spelling

Larry Mollin, who helped craft my character,
Kelly Taylor, on *Beverly Hills, 90210*, hasn't lost
his touch with this teen romance thriller,
which is set—you guessed it—in Beverly Hills.

—Jennie Garth

THE Pool Guy's Kid

Also by Larry Mollin

Search: Paul Clayton (2018)

St. Malo (2019)

Cayuga (2020)

Road to Shambala (2022)

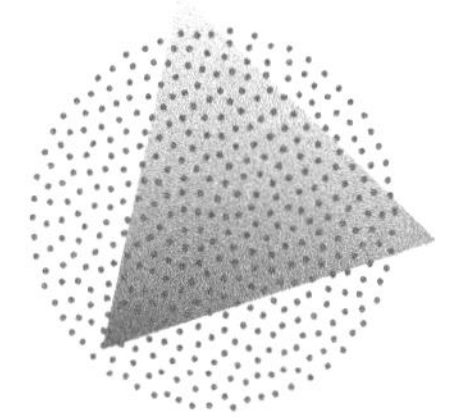

THE Pool Guy's Kid

A NOVEL

LARRY MOLLIN

Shadelandhouse
MODERN PRESS

Lexington, Kentucky

A Shadelandhouse Modern Press book
The Pool Guy's Kid
A novel

The Pool Guy's Kid is a work of fiction. Characters, incidents, names, and places are used fictitiously or are products of the author's imagination. Any resemblance to actual events, locales, organizations, or persons, living or dead, is entirely coincidental. Any references to real places are used fictitiously. To the extent any trademarks, service marks, product names, or named features are used in this work of fiction, all are assumed to be the property of their respective owners and are used only for reference. Use of these terms does not imply endorsement.

Published in the United States of America by:
Shadelandhouse Modern Press, LLC
Lexington, Kentucky
smpbooks.com

First edition 2024

Shadelandhouse, Shadelandhouse Modern Press,
and the logo are trademarks of Shadelandhouse Modern Press, LLC.

ISBN: 978-1-945049-42-2 (paperback) ISBN: 978-1-945049-46-0 (epub)
Library of Congress Control Number: applied for

Cover and book design: iota books
Cover art and interior illustrations: Annelisa Hermosilla
Author photo: Jackson Mollin

for the loyal fans of
beverly hills, 90210
around the world.

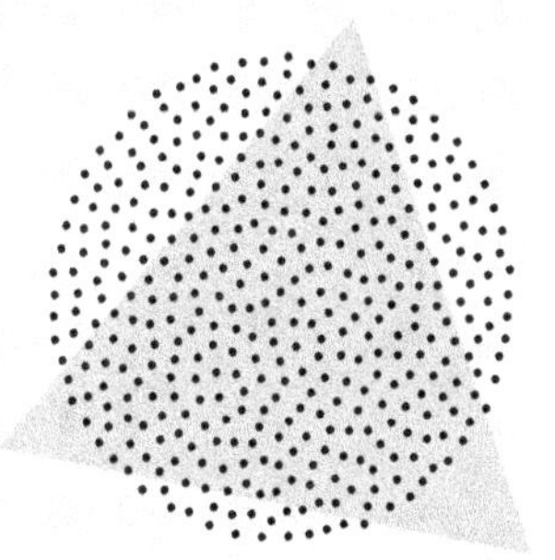

AEUrA

right Now

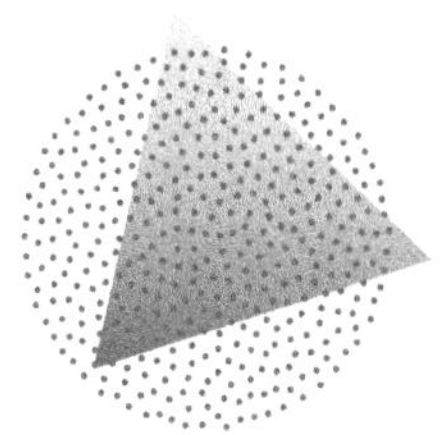

there are 2,612 backyard swimming pools in beverly hills. The city has more pools per capita than any other city in the world. My dad services maybe twenty-four or twenty-five of them a week. Maybe because occasionally the clients' monthly payments come to an abrupt stop. It happens. He's been known to say, *In Beverly Hills, people go tits up or join the underground.* He has no filter, also no ambition. It's enough that most of his steady customers like and trust him. He works in the self-proclaimed "garden spot of the world," but he is straight working-class West LA. His name is Duke Montrose, and I have the enviable position of being his only kid, Gilly.

There's a lot of time to kill before daylight and while I don't have an internet signal, as I'm hiding inside this junked, five-hundred–gallon propane tank, I do have a voice recorder and a full charge on my iPhone 14, which is finally paid for. If it goes tits up for me, this recording may be all that survives, so listen on.

A little background:

I go to University High—like my father did—and hope to graduate come June. After that (if there is a *that*) who knows? I earn my keep in the rent-controlled, two-bedroom Duke and I share on Olympic and Bentley by helping him do pools after school.

Correct. It sucks.

So it was no surprise when I got a text from him before sixth period. The Duke was stuck on the other side of the hill, in the San Fernando Valley, looking for a used pool heater and more discount chemicals. He needed me to cover the only job of the day. It was a rental house behind the Beverly Hills Hotel, at the end of Laurel Way, with a saltwater infinity monster and an equally huge Jacuzzi. A two-man job. Would I rather be hanging out after school playing *Fortnite* and debating Leticia Almora on the merits of being my Senior Dance date? If only.

None of what happens this late November afternoon is Duke's fault. I want to make that clear. I have to, as this could be my last word and testament. Our plan now is to wait till sunup and sneak out, try to get back over the hill, and find someone in the Beverly Hills police force who believes us. I did say *us*. I am not alone in this dark, empty tank that the Duke once rigged for a bachelor party gag in this Sun Valley scrapyard. I am with Aeura Kim, pronounced *Aura*. *She* is visiting from Houston, looking at colleges, and we've hardly known each other two days, though it seems like a lifetime. Her dad, Mr. Sidney Kim, is being held by the police for murder, and we are the only ones besides the killers who know he is being framed. Is that as corny as it sounds? I hope not because it is true.

thurſday, two days ago

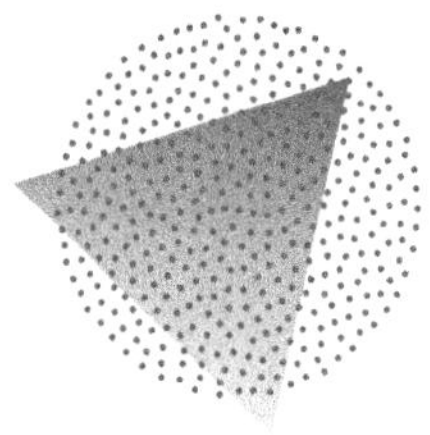

After i got that afternoon text from duke, I shot one off to VJ, my good friend and auxiliary pool-cleaning helper. He's third-generation Japanese American. Lives off Sawtelle and Tennessee in the same house from which his great-grandparents were ripped and put into a detention camp during World War II. It's next to the family nursery the government returned. VJ is a senior like me, an academic hotshot unlike me, and on the debate team, which happens to be the best club for meeting girls if you are not an athlete, says my boy VJ. I joined as a promise to my mom, Julieta, whom I miss every day. A car crash almost two years back put her underground. Everything that's classy about me comes from my Chilean-born mother. She had me reading Lorca poetry when I was twelve. Funny, reading Lorca was what first caught my eye about Aeura. Mom's angel hand at work?

Duke was known all over the Westside for his tricked-out, red, 1964 Ranchero. He had parked it on the bad side of the road for street cleaning day. Such was the Duke's parking karma that he almost never got a ticket. Of course, he was an occasional bedmate of the meter maid so there was that. The old pickup was his pride and joy, stolen more than once, always magically coming back better. Duke called it his *car-ma*. Me and VJ loaded it at the storage shed at the back of our six-unit apartment building. It was conveniently close to the unemployment office, Duke loved to point out. He was looking forward to retiring at fifty. More so, since he was already fifty-five, too young for Medicare and Social Security. Lack of these entitlements haunted him deeply and prevented him from the agony of doing the bills. That became my job too. Don't get sad for me. I have my fun, my own money and hopes—not to mention, one immediate desire, make that a prayer, that the goons who followed us from Glendale haven't found Duke's truck where we abandoned it under the pile of old palm fronds on this junkyard boulevard, in the shithole of the Valley. Let me slow down so you get the whole picture of what went down during that job.

* * *

Heading to the hills of Beverly, VJ and I went true north on Sepulveda and took Sunset east to Whittier Drive to Lexington to Benedict Canyon and then Laurel Way. I laughed thinking of Duke's favorite *Saturday Night Live* sketch, "The Californians." It was an LA soap opera where between intrigue and romance all the characters were obsessed with finding the best route to avoid traffic. VJ, who was a Waze app junkie, didn't get the joke. We rolled up to the estate and things took an unfortunate turn. New security at the service gate stopped us and asked us to get out. This was an elite property owned by an old Uni High classmate of Duke's who had made a killing in real estate before he was thirty. A lost opportunity for the Dukester to have partnered early on. When he would get really low, *mi padre* would beat himself up about this blown chance. For years the estate has operated as a top-end, month-to-month leaser, while Duke's bud lived an even higher life year-round in Majorca. He could afford better pool cleaners than Duke, but he was loyal and occasionally would give Duke stock tips that hit. The property attracted the superrich and beautiful, and usually there was a party atmosphere for the Oscars or the Grammys or some other Beverly Hills hoo-ha. Today it felt different.

No party was going on. The new tenants' security was a prime cut above rent-a-cop and had the custom-tailored suit to shout it out. Thoughtfully Duke had complied with their instructions and had forwarded my ID ahead to the swarthy, hard-bodied guard at the back gate. It was my DMV photo from when I was sixteen, short haired, still pudgy, and shorter. Not tall, handsome, and buff like I am now. Unhear that—I don't want to jinx it.

Mr. Suspicious, whom I later learned was named Rob Hartunian, looked me up and down, wanded me with care, and gave an okay nod. VJ, however, got no nod. The *hardo* wouldn't even look at his ID. VJ was not on the entry list and wasn't getting in. Duke had neglected to send VJ's ID, saying he thought I would. Another lame excuse, as if I knew the number to the service gate. On the phone with Duke, I could tell he was at a bar waiting for the rush-hour gridlock to die down. This was going to be a job from hell for one person. I begged him to reschedule, but Duke said they had guests and it had to be done.

He said he'd make it up to me. I knew he would. Duke wasn't the worst dad.

I paid off VJ for his time cause that's how I roll and got him a rideshare. With the time change, the sun was already hanging low. I parked the truck as close to the pool area as I could and started shlepping the gear in, two hand trucks' worth. I was not alone. The closer I got to poolside, the clearer I could hear young girls giggling from one of the closed cabanas. The two stuck out their heads as if on cue and giggled some more at the sight of me. They were Korean for sure, maybe fifteen or younger. Learning in a diversity hub like Uni, I can tell. VJ had schooled me hard. These kids were straight out of that K-pop world and flaunting it. They had the black bang cuts, cool T-shirts, and plaid schoolgirl miniskirts.

Better that VJ wasn't here, or like a bad loser, he'd be going off about Koreans. He can't get over the fact now Korea—not Japan—makes the best movies, TV sets, and cars. For centuries Koreans were treated as the lowest rung of the Asian pecking order, the absolute bottom, a mongrel race. Like Bolivians to my mother's South American friends. People always feel better when they have someone else to dump on. *Way of the world,* says Duke.

I got to it, unpacked the necessities, and was in a good working rhythm with a wired headset feeding me a Malcolm Gladwell–type podcast that Leticia had recommended about social media and children under twelve. It was an upcoming debate club topic, and I committed to take the pro side to defend it. Next fall Leticia was probably headed to UCLA on a scholarship where her mother was a professor of economics. She had a real look of success, a damn head turner, too, when she tried. I was aiming high, punching above my weight, according to dear old dad. If he's the king of low expectations, what does that make me, the prince? To date I am not sure if Leticia is grooming me for something or is falling in love.

With the podcast's pedantic arguments grating on my ears, I did my thing—Jacuzzi first, ran the saltwater analysis, and spied another Korean girl. This one in a ponytail, sweatshirt, and yoga pants, reading a book inside another cabana at the diving board end of the pool. I almost fell into the water angling to double-check the book title, which was *Collected Poems of Federico García Lorca.* I wanted to give a thumbs-up, but a terrified squeal got me running to help. It was one of the K-pop twins. Her Bluetooth earbud had popped out of an earring-laden lobe and had landed under the hardscape's French drain. Oh the tragedy. Agitated, as if facing death itself, she communicated in Korean. I got the gist, knelt down face to the ground, and did the necessary dirty work. The pod was wedged in and took a little time and careful maneuvering to free it whole. While I was rescuing it for them, they were filming behind my back, my butt crack flashing. I only found this out later from Aeura who predicts the little pop tarts will put it on TikTok. My butt jiggling double speed to an EDM track? Aeura thinks it will go viral. Joy.

The pool wasn't going to clean itself. I got back to balancing the pH factor, acid base ratio, using my twelfth-grade math and science acumen. Perfect. Duke insisted that this part of the job be spot on. This was always easier to calculate and correct here than it was in the older chlorine pools we serviced. We had to use those chemicals with even more care. They were poison. Skull-and-crossbones stuff. You wore gloves and a mask on those calls, or it could screw with your skin and lungs.

Cleaning pools is a good workout. My muscles are toned, and I was stripped to a T-shirt in the last sunlight of the day. With my LA Dodgers hat on backward I was feeling maximum cool, which doesn't happen often. In that golden time before dusk, flaunting my dip net skill at debris retrieval as I skimmed the sparkling saltwater pool along its edges, I noticed my hand truck on the back path. My chemical box for non-saltwater jobs was not there. While packing up, had I left the old black milk crate with the big plastic jug of chlorine back in the shed? That seemed logical. I would not have needed it. But still…

* * *

(Flash forward to right now, a few nights later, doing this recording. I did not leave the chemicals in the shed. VJ confirmed that. I should have paid more attention to my gut at the time, but I had work to do and not much daylight.)

* * *

The four drains were clean except for a Skittles wrapper and some nail-polish–stained Q-tips. Happy me, they took no time at all. I started the vacuum scrub at the pool's deep end and put my heart into it, switching out of the podcast and into a playlist that reflected Duke's musical influence. The first song to welcome me on shuffle was Derek and the Dominos's "Why Does Love Got to Be So Sad?" I wondered about Leticia and me. So far we had not even kissed. I mean, we…she held back, okay. I got the message and have patience. Why does love have to be so sad?

At the other end of the pool area an older Asian woman emerged from the house in a bathrobe. She waved me over, and I got the spa up and running for her as she had asked. I set the heat at 103 degrees, which is optimum for an ideal Jacuzzi experience, quoth the Duke. The woman, wearing a two-piece bathing suit, laid out on a chaise longue while the spa heated up. She was maybe Duke's age and would fit in at any shop in

Beverly Hills, with the amount of plastic surgery to her face and figure. She thanked me in accent-thick English, and I could tell she was very nervous. I thought it was about me and tried to work faster and finish up. That was it. The whole time I spent with Delores Sung, who would be dead by evening.

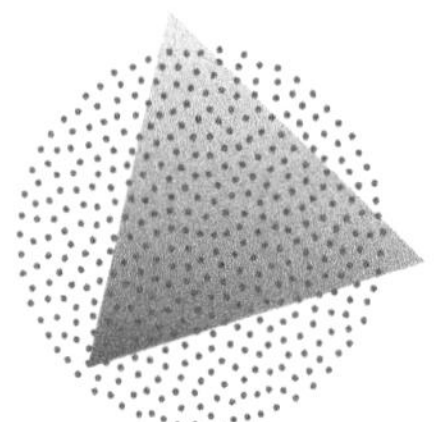

3.

rigHt Now

I cannot see Aeura's eyes inside the junked propane tank, but her voice has an urgency that can't be denied. It was going to happen sooner or later. We'd already been hiding out for hours. I stop my recording and check the time—3:20 a.m. Pocketing the device, I open the tank's top hatch that Duke had custom-made for a bachelor party's surprise stripper. I peek around, head barely out, like I'm expecting gunfire. Am I being too dramatic?

It's dark and quiet AF in this junkyard that's been our salvation. I see ghostly rows of disassembled autos, auto parts, discarded appliances, and of course, propane tanks. The yard's owned by an old poker buddy of Duke's who is huge in the scrap-metal world. Another winner who makes Duke feel like a loser. A guy—not unlike Duke—who broke through the working-class ceiling and lives large up on Roscomare in Bel Air. The fresh air is intoxicating. I help Aeura climb out. We both disappear as nature calls. We'd snuck under the yard's barbwire fence to get inside. I think we can slip out the same way and get the truck. For the first time in a while my phone connects and dings with notifications. I mute it and hold my breath. They're from Duke, except one from VJ. Duke's messages are all cursing that I took the truck and the police had come by. Why am I not surprised? VJ's text is all in caps:

GET OFFLINE AND KILL CELLULAR, DUDE, THEY CAN TRACK YOU!

4.

thursday, two days ago

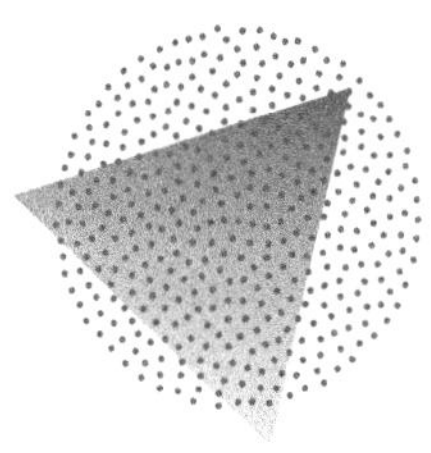

AƐURA KIM WAS ON BREAK FROM A PRIVATE SCHOOL IN HOUSTON where she was a junior. She lived with her divorced mother there and, unlike her father's partner's vacationing K-kids from Seoul, she'd been in America for the last ten of her seventeen years. She spoke English with a slight British accent from her time in Hong Kong. Her hair was clipped short, and the heavy, dark eye makeup set her apart as a goth, emo, intellectual-type outlier of Korean descent. I noticed none of this on first seeing her covered up with a hoodie and sweats. All I noticed was her choice of reading. Before I left the property I dragged some hose by her cabana and remarked on the Lorca book. I assumed that like the K-pop twins she wasn't from this country. She didn't help matters by looking at me blankly and nodding without speaking a word back. The older woman on the chaise seemed to be watching us, and I got that vibe again to cut it short and keep moving. Before I finished hauling gear and repacking the truck, the moon was rising with a mocking smile on the lowly like me who toil for the rich and useless. I was off to catch up with Leticia about debate stuff and keep working her angles. Duke would be back soon and if past is prologue, he would have gone to Chili John's chili house in Burbank and picked us up a few quarts of deliciousness. It all seemed suddenly promising. Before I could start the engine, she tapped on the passenger window.

Can I grab a ride with you to West Hollywood? Book Soup.

-Sure, hop in.

What was I going to say? Sorry, hard pass.

Dressed now like the rebel she is, Aeura got in with a backpack and a twinkle. The Ranchero's rebored V-8 jumped to life. Across the pool area, a uniformed maid came charging down the service path toward the truck, waving her hands and calling.

Miss Aeura! No! Stay here! You must stay!

-Go! Go!

I went, went at Aeura's command. Was it wrong? Probably. Aeura ducked down in her seat, and we shot out the back gate before the guard noticed. Down Laurel Way I did ask the obvious.

Am I going to catch heat for this?

-I'll pay you for any trouble.

Okay.

Book Soup? I couldn't let her go in alone. It's one of the coolest bookstores in LA. My mother took me there several times to hear authors and get her books signed. She loved the classic poets—Browning, Keats, and Dickinson—but she kept up with the latest. I got to meet the great Billy Collins at Book Soup. Search him online. She wouldn't read Bukowski though, too sexist, and urged me not to—which of course made me a fan. I parked in a loading zone on Sunset and introduced myself to my passenger.

I'm Gilly. Short for Guillermo.

-Aeura. Pronounced Aura.

Sweet. Let's go find you some books.

5.

riqHt Now

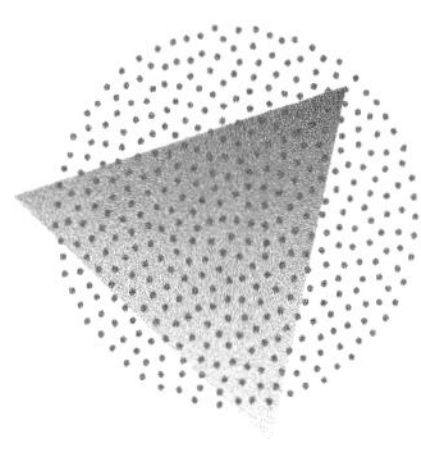

i doN't WANt to pANic AeurA, but I have to get her back into our hiding place. If VJ is right, the killers after us could be camped out by the truck. We need to wait at least until daylight. In the dark of the confined space, I can hear her crying. She interrupts our silence.

Don't say anything.

-It's alright to—

I'm not crying.

Right. I reach for her and give her a comforting, brotherly

hug. Aeura dissolves into my arms, head buried deep in my shoulder. I can feel the wetness of her tears. Or was that a kiss? My heart is racing. I can hear hers beating harder over her whisper.

I am so sorry I got you into this.

That apology is of little comfort if we can't survive the night. I don't say that—or anything—which I think she appreciates. Instead, I focus on our options, starting with the Beverly Hills police. They are holding Aeura's father for the death of his second wife, Delores Sung. Aeura and I are wanted as *persons of interest*, insane as that sounds. More on that later. Seeking Duke's help would be no help and worse. To get in touch with him could put him in jeopardy. The people behind this are in deep. Billions or bust. They have already killed two people, set up a fall guy with a motive, and planted evidence. It would be our word against theirs if we are lucky enough to stay above ground and speak truth to power.

Aeura is nodding off. I will keep documenting.

thurſday, two dayſ ago

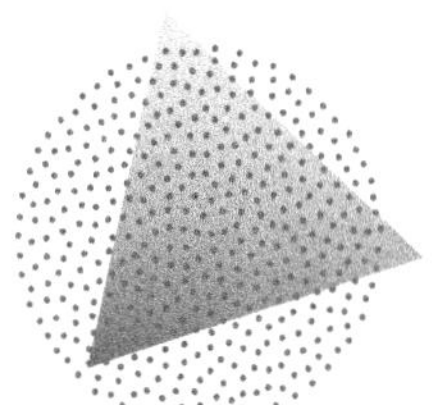

tHere waſ magic iN tHe bookſtore on Sunset Boulevard that evening. The clerk was new to me. He was a wizard, a word nerd to the   . Aeura was looking for an older saga about five generations of an Afghan family and found it without knowing the title or author, thanks to Owen Lattimer. Aeura had some wicked fun trying to stump the UCLA world lit major. Owen was loving the attention and aiming high. I respected that and left them laughing about John Kennedy Toole while I searched for a book of my own.

Aeura had told me to pick any one I wanted and it was on her. I couldn't decide between a Richard Lange or a John Fante novel and then had an epiphany. If I could have one book it might as well be something in hard cover. Otherwise, I'd rather have another file on my Kindle. Unlike my mom I am a digital media consumer and proud of it–on-demand books, movies, and music. I only come to Book Soup once in a while for the vibe. I picked out a dream coffee-table book. Rock star images from Beverly Hills's own Guy Webster, a pioneer record album photographer and old friend of Duke's, long gone. It was a worthy treasure, and Aeura approved. When Owen rang us up I could see he and Aeura had made a connection. Was I the only one watching them?

(Speculation: Book Soup was not where Aeura was supposed to be in this murder plot of her father's business partners. All the traces of her absence from the Laurel Way house needed to be erased. Including me. Including Owen.)

At the bookstore, Owen, despite the desire percolating inside him, couldn't escape the fact Aeura's credit card was not going through. No matter how many times he tried, he couldn't ring up our stuff. Without cash on her it was me who saved Aeura the embarrassment and paid for it all with a debit card. Owen bagged us up and invited us to an LA Poet Society reading the following night. When we both said we'd come he made a funny about uninviting me. He was cute, all in for Aeura, and I feel so guilty, and nothing will change that. If I had gotten his phone call earlier maybe Owen would still be alive.

Outside, Aeura thanked me and on the spot, Venmoed me all the money I had laid out, plus a generous $500 more. I hit the bank transfer button to ACCEPT as quickly as I could. The exchange went through. Glory be. I felt like I won the lottery.

It was all downhill from there.

7.

right Now

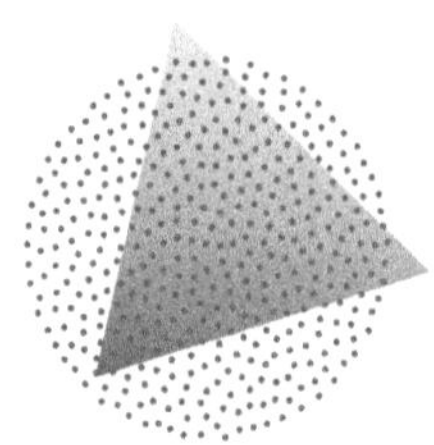

it's ALMost 4 A.M. Aeura is Asleep, head in my lap. I am hoping our pursuers have called off the search and have gone to bed themselves. I am sure Aeura's father's business partners, James Hyung of Seoul and Rodney Allan of Beverly Hills, are wide awake and scheming. They successfully set up their former partner, Sidney Kim, as the only suspect in the death of Delores Sung—his wife and Aeura's stepmother. Now they need to silence us before their crypto-mining IPO hits the market next week. Why Glendale goons are helping them I can only imagine.

(Speculation: Aeura says the American partner is a high roller, a gambler. Her father and stepmother had argued about the source of their company's bridge financing. Maybe the Armenian mob provided that and is protecting their investment.)

We have to make a move soon, and it has to be the right one. For now this tank is home, a womb where we are safe. Recording starting again at 4:02 a.m. Where was I?

8.

thurſday, two nightſ ago

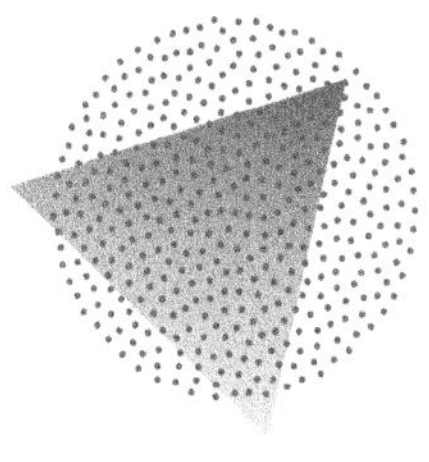

on the ride back from book ſoup, I gave Aeura a tour guide's cruise of West Hollywood's Sunset Strip. It was somewhat depressing for me. A lot of my favorites are gone, including the House of Blues that Duke got me into regularly when I was a tween. Rock and roll, blues and soul, fare thee well. It was replaced by the luxury hotel Pendry West and a trendy escape room attraction. Traveling west we passed the Whiskey a Go Go. It still holds the corner at Clark Street and Sunset Boulevard where it's been since the '60s. Aeura knew all about the LA punk music scene that started there. More than me. She teased my punk and emo ignorance, which I took as a badge of honor. It was a decent cruise, cool. I didn't feel an attraction to her. It wasn't like that. Aeura was good company, interesting, funny in her negative way of seeing things. She hated most everything popular. She told me she wanted to be a journalist so she could expose bullshit wherever she found it. She had started a bullshit-detecting blog that attracted some followers till her father asked her to stop until after his company's IPO went through.

VJ texted me during the ride to let me know the debate club officers, namely he and Leticia, would be at the Westwood Starbucks around 8 p.m. I planned to drop off Aeura, drop off Duke's truck, and make it on time. I am known for being on time. It was drilled into me by my mother. She had been an actress in Chilean theater and was trained with that discipline. We turned on Benedict, passed the Beverly Hills Hotel, passed Lexington Road, made the left at sleepy old Laurel Way, and— what the hell, there was backed up traffic. News vans, a fire engine, Beverly Hills Police Department (BHPD) cars, and an ambulance. Aeura was in a panic.

Let me out!

Without another word, she threw open the truck door and fled. Forgetting about her bag of books and me, she hurried down the lane through the hive of emergency personnel. When I last saw her that night she was rushing into the arms of an older Asian man—her father, no doubt. They walked away. I waited for a bit, feeling helpless, in the way, like a fool rubbernecking freeway wreckage. I figured I could drop off her bag at a better time. I took off with my Guy Webster coffee-table book and $500 more in my debit account. Even Duke would high-five that.

* * *

Duke had the Chili John's rocking in the pan when I came in. I changed on the move. Washing up, I opted not to shave. No point. Unlikely a night for me and Leticia to share a first kiss. Duke asked about the work at Laurel Way. I started off telling him about the color-coordinated K-pop twins, and he was amused. It's always a crapshoot owning a high-end rental, Duke avowed. Not that he owned any, but he always sounded like a real estate expert. I let him get away with it, something I had learned to do. Scarfing down the good grub, I relaxed and enjoyed it. It was obvious he had not heard anything about the emergency at the property from his bud, the owner. I did not bring it up. If I did, I never would have gotten out of the house. That was wrong, and I hope to hell Duke does not pay somehow because I didn't tell him right away. Instead, I Venmoed him my rent and grabbed my lightweight BMX bike from the shed. The milk crate with a jug and chemicals was nowhere in sight. In denial, I packed away that weirdness in the back of my head and padlocked the shed, pedaling off to Westwood.

VJ and Leticia were nursing their Frappuccinos when I strolled in, my sun-bleached long hair still damp from the shower. I was feeling pretty spiffy in an almost-new Burberry sweater, black jeans, new Vans. I look older than eighteen, everyone says. VJ had to comment on my overdressing for the meeting, and I couldn't tell if Leticia saw me blushing. Leticia was organized AF and gave us a hard copy of the rundown for the debate match against the hated Beverly Hills High the next day. The social media issue was going to be the penultimate match. No pressure, Gilly. I had absorbed a good bit of the super-relevant podcast and had some views of my own. I was confident AF. Leticia seemed turned on by that. I was thinking that I should have shaved, when my cell rang, harshing my mellow. It was Duke. His friend had called. A woman had died in the Laurel Way Jacuzzi. WTF!?

9.

rigHt Now

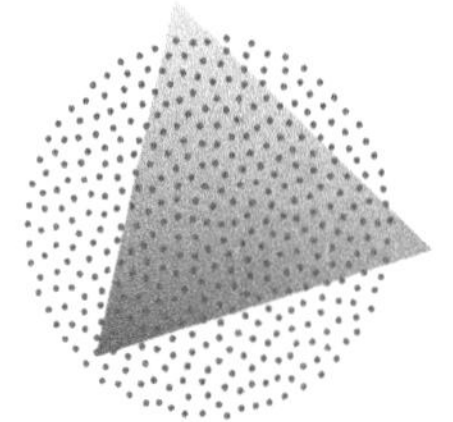

it'r a few Hourr before dAwN and black as night outside and inside this godsend of a salvaged gas tank. The only illumination is the display screen on my phone. It's amazing when you are off the internet how little battery charge you use. I can speak out loud since Aeura is sound asleep, head still in my lap, snoring. Her hair smells good. I am big on smell and I like the scent of her. I can only imagine how pissed off at me Leticia will be. VJ at least understands why I ditched the debate before the end. As tempting as it is to make a call, I am afraid. The criminals behind this murder and cover-up have deep hooks into the authorities, and they have money—lots of money, according to Aeura. Her father is no saint either. A mathematician by trade, he married his second wife, the late Delores Sung, and she provided the fortune he needed to develop the unique crypto-mining start-up that became the company. The out-of-the box concept is what attracted the Korean partner and subsequently the American partner, Rodney Allan. Sidney was skeptical of Rodney.

Delores more so. It was no secret there was tension between the partners as the IPO and its potential bounty loomed. Also there was downright hostility between Sidney and Delores, who threatened to divorce him. The night Aeura arrived from Houston, she witnessed a domestic squabble that bordered on a physical confrontation between them. Rodney, whom Aeura found creepy, had seen it as well.

Delores had surprised Sidney by flying in from Macau to join him in Beverly Hills, supposedly to help with the IPO launch. She wanted to plan the party. Sidney was not pleased. At first Aeura thought he was being protective of her, his only child, knowing she and Delores did not get along at all. A phone call to Aeura's mother in Texas gave a reason—her father probably had a mistress just like he did when he and her mother were married. Aeura had to hang up before her mom ranted on. She usually believed only half of what her mother said about her father, but this time her mother may have been one hundred percent accurate.

There are a lot of angles in here that I do not understand or much want to. My decision to help Aeura, in retrospect, is dumb. My life's horizon could be shrinking. Now I have to own it. I better record the events of yesterday while they are still fresh in my mind. Here goes.

friday, yesterday

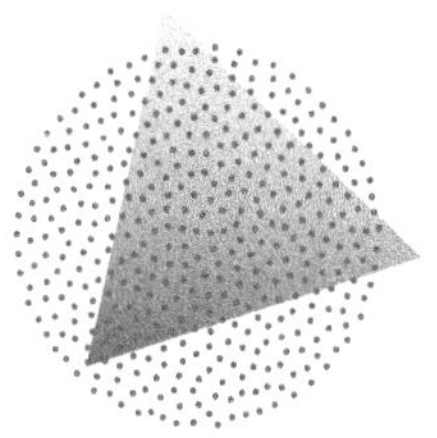

AFTER DUKE RELAYED THE SCANT INFO HE GOT ABOUT THE DEATH ON LAUREL WAY, I excused myself from Leticia and VJ and biked off from the Starbucks, my head spinning. Duke was gone when I got home. The note he left mentioned meeting a friend at Fantasy Island. Not the TV series, a local gentlemen's club that Duke used as an occasional office. He added that I shouldn't concern myself with the clients. *Nothing to do with us, okay?* With no way to find out more about how Delores died, I tried to sleep and finally did. In the morning I was up with the sun, grabbing that bag of Aeura's books and the keys to Duke's truck. He wouldn't be up till later. I was going to leave the books at the security gate, drop back the truck, and bike over to school before homeroom. It seemed doable.

The scene at Laurel Way was still buzzing. There were no fire trucks or ambulances, but there were police vehicles and CSI techs moving around with blue gloves and yellow crime tape closing access to the front gate. I braved it as far as I was allowed. Hartunian, the guard who had given me and VJ that difficult time, was on the inside of the yellow tape. I got his attention and held up the bag, hoping he would help. What was I thinking? The big man did not give me a second look. He was focused on the driveway where the police were leading off Mr. Sidney Kim in cuffs while Aeura was yelling and trying to pull him away. A policewoman took hold of her as her father was lowered into the back seat of a police car and driven off. I was frozen, hoping Aeura would notice me. A slick, Asian tycoon, whom I later would learn was James Hyung, put a comforting arm around Aeura. She tossed it off and bolted for the gate. I waved.

Aeura!

She didn't make it. The gate guard stopped her and pulled her back, kicking and screaming up the driveway. I yelled in her defense. A BHPD policeman came over and tried to calm me down. He wasn't much older than me, and he was decent. He listened to his earpiece and explained Aeura was being taken to the station to be questioned. It was routine. He didn't have to explain but like I said, he was decent. I wish I had noticed his name. I watched a plainclothes cop who looked to be in charge take over and with the policewoman helping, they got Aeura into his dark Lexus. The young patrolman moved the tape so the car could exit. He looked over at me.

Your girlfriend?

-No. I...never mind.

As the Lexus passed me, I held up the Book Soup bag for Aeura to see. Too late to realize how lame that must have looked to her, considering how things were going. I didn't figure that when I held the bag up, it also caught the eye of the gate goon, Hartunian, and made me and the lovestruck book clerk targets. If Aeura was in West Hollywood buying books, how could she have been helping her father kill her stepmother, Delores, at the same time? Desperate people like Aeura's father's partners do desperate things. Especially when they are in bed with mobsters. The fix was supposed to be in. We were the *poop in the pool*, as Duke would say.

I didn't know any of that at the time and got myself back on schedule. Dropped off the truck and made it to first period. VJ wanted to know everything, and between classes I filled him in. By fifth period I had rethought it all out and told him that it was better, safer, to forget it all. Timing is everything and mine has been pitiful. Leticia tried to talk to me before AP English. She was excited about our debate team meet, and I was too. I was going to crush it and earn that first kiss. Before I could even give her my best face forward, the vice principal motioned me to the office. The detective from this morning was here to take me in for questioning. More WTF?!

A walk of shame ensued. Kids craning their necks from classrooms to see me walking down the halls with Detective Joe Boylan of the Beverly Hills Police Department. I could tell photos were being grabbed and postings on social media would follow. I put my sweatshirt hood over my head, but that only made it look worse. I lowered the hood and took the heat. It hit me as strange, even then, that a homicide detective would come himself to bring me in for questioning. I was not a suspect—or was I? And if I was, wouldn't there be at least a uniformed cop with him? Didn't feel right. And why did Leticia have to witness it? There she was, with a look and a headshake that said to me, *Why do I bother with you?* That was deadening.

I better stop recording. Aeura is awake and—hold on. She just kissed me in the dark, and my ears are ringing.

right now

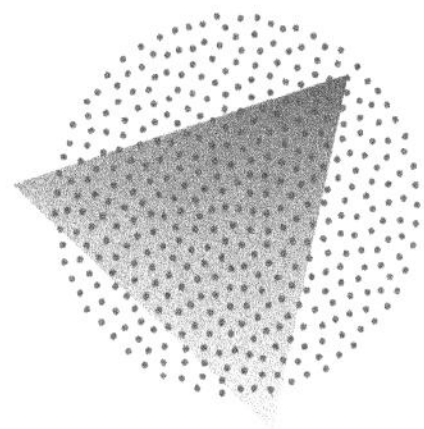

thank you, gilly. you are my only.

-*Only what?*

Only only. You saved me.

She kisses me again in the dark, cramped space. Her body's warmth radiates through me, and I need it bad. Her lips are the softest, puffiest cushions and seem electrified. I hold her even tighter and kiss her back till her ears are ringing. Leticia be damned! I am in no position to continue recording. That will have to wait. Aeura is cold, and I can't and won't let go of her.

Gilly, what if today was the last of our lives?

-Whoa. Let's not go there. The sun's up. We can—

She takes my hand and holds it to her pounding heart. Her eyes pour into mine. Her skin feels like quicksilver *en fuego* under my hand. She leans in to kiss me with her tongue darting deep in my mouth, a desperate longing, for the longest time. Then the kiss breaks and we catch the same breath. It's heaven. It's hell. A sudden fit of coughing engulfs us at the same time. We are wracked and gasping. Not cool. Something is burning!

Something really is on fire! Peeking out the gas tank portal, I can't see the sun though it must be up. The smell of gasoline stings as much as the smoke that covers the salvage yard. Flames are crackling as a hazy, brutish figure in the distance dumps out more gasoline. The mobsters have set the yard on fire. We have to flee or be cooked! Now!

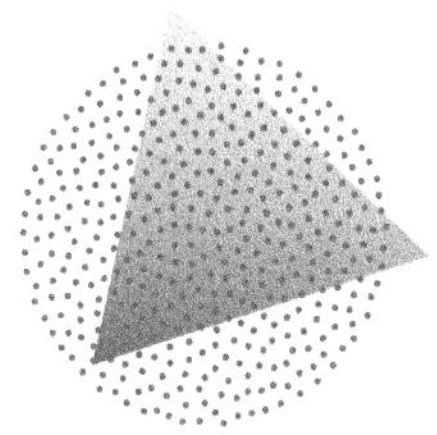

friday, yesterday

detective boylan sat me in the front seat of
his black lexus, and off we went. I tried to relax and be
as polite as I could. Things got screwy when we drove right by
the Beverly Hills police building. I didn't say anything. Boylan
started dissing Uni High kids not even being fit to take out the
trash at Beverly Hills High where he graduated. *What a loser*, I
thought, despite the five-figure Piaget watch he sported. Cops
and real estate agents in Beverly Hills always try to impress.
Boylan parked illegally in a blue-lined, accessible spot at La

Cienega Park at the east end of the city. I could feel the hair on the back of my neck bristle. This was not what I expected. Boylan, who looked to be Duke's age, got to the core of the matter.

You're in big trouble, Guillermo. Chemicals you used in the spa contributed to the death of Delores Sung. Did Sidney Kim ask you to do it? Or did you give him the chlorine jug? Free shot here if you answer now. Were you in on it?

-What? No! Do I need a lawyer?

Duke had a married, female friend, an Inglewood lawyer, who handled his DUI and became a trusted, occasional booty call. Boylan put his hand on me to quell my fears.

No. You don't need a lawyer.

-Good. Cause I didn't use chlorine. The Laurel Way property is saltwater.

Boylan said he knew that, though I doubted it. He was going to do me a big favor. He could tell I wasn't involved, just careless, he said, in leaving it around.

The victim was overcome by chlorine fumes, fell backward, and sustained a fatal head injury on the spa's rock edge. At least that's what the killer hoped we'd believe. Coroner considered it an overdose of chlorine. Maybe half a gallon poured into the Jacuzzi.

-No way.

Yes way.

-Crazy!

He patted my shoulder with a reassuring tap and told me he'd keep me out of it. They had the victim's husband and his daughter. Old man snapped at the wife and then tried to cover it up with his daughter's help and blame you.

Boylan was looking for me to thank him. Seriously.

I don't think so. Aeura, his daughter, was with me.

-Huh? Keep that to yourself for now. Got it?

I nodded that I did. He checked his sick watch and told me to get out. If I was lucky, I wouldn't see him again. What a dick.

How am I supposed to get back to school?

-You're a smart guy. Figure it out.

He pulled off with a squeal and headed west into the city. I was off for the nearest bus stop when my muted cell buzzed in my back pocket. It was Aeura. She was calling from the restroom of an attorney's office. She'd been taken there after being questioned by the police. Her father's lawyer had won her release, but now she thinks she's been kidnapped.

Gilly, can you come get me?

Before I could answer, she texted me a Glendale address. Glendale? Who in Beverly Hills would be represented by a lawyer from the East Valley? I texted back telling her I had school, added some clasped hand emojis, and sent it. I hoped she didn't think that was too weird. With no reply, I got on the #6 bus down Olympic Boulevard. School was going to be almost over by the time I got back. The debate meet still seemed possible. It would be a little sketchy showing up after missing classes, but I had a good excuse. I tried to concentrate on my "social media is healthy" argument. As the bus passed through Beverly Hills my phone chimed with a notification. It was a Venmo transaction. Money intended for my account was waiting for my approval—a lot of money, with payment described "for RESCUE."

13.

rigHt Now

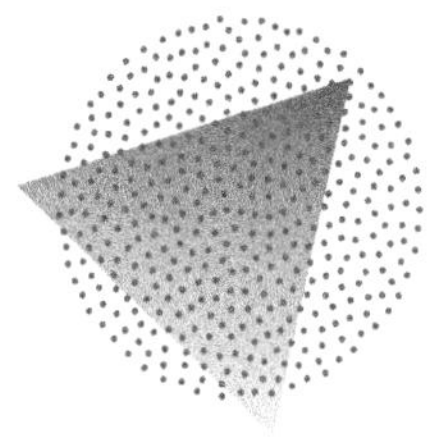

it's so Hot. the Lot is oN fire. The smell is overbearing. We crawl single file away from the flames, below the smoke line. Aeura is behind me. I have been to this junkyard a few times and have an idea where the back fence is. The lot is on an east-west boulevard, and we are making our way south where a high, wire-mesh boundary lines an alley and a chance at escape. There won't be a hole beneath it to crawl through, only chain link and nasty hooked wire. Despite the dirty haze, lightning flashes crackle from the heavens. We look up. Who says it never rains in

California? It can pour—and please, let it rip. Thunder booms.

Yes! Our faces feel the fat, wet drops, and we quicken our pace. I am wearing a jean jacket and take it off at the back fence. The heat is intense. The dampened smoke is a welcome screen shielding us. There's only one way out. Up.

Can you climb?

-Watch me.

Aeura wriggles off her leather jacket and tosses it over the top of the fence where it catches a section of barbed wire. I do the same. She hesitates.

It's going to hurt, isn't it?

-Less than being roasted.

She goes for it, clambering high to the top. I see the jagged wire catching flesh on her back as she vaults over. She doesn't scream. Now it's my turn. I am halfway up the fence when a gunshot rings out nearby. I hurry to the crest and take the penetrating pain of the razor wire to get over. I hit the ground hard, rolling over the rough gravel of the alley. I am out! I am bleeding. Aeura is bleeding. Ever near, fire sirens are going off for real, and also in my head with an alarming idea. We can surrender ourselves to a fire station like abandoned newborns needing safe haven. We may be okay that way and buy time. We move into the alley shadows behind a broken-down RV to tend to our wounds and wait for a chance to turn ourselves in. One thing to me is crystal clear. This could all have been avoided if I had stayed at the debate.

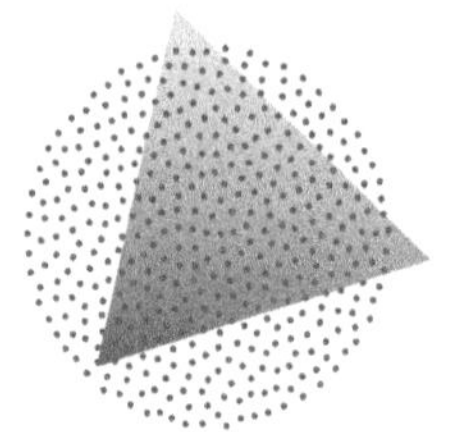

friday, yesterday

i didN't Accept AeurA's geNerous offer waiting for me in the Venmo app on my phone. At that moment I was too overwhelmed by the fear of what I might be getting into. Coupled with Detective Boylan's warning, there seemed to be a risk even talking to anyone about this. The circle of trust was limited to Aeura and me, and I felt lost at how to proceed. I settled back on the bus ride till I was close enough to school to walk the rest of the way. It didn't help that I played a voicemail I'd missed while I was with Detective Boylan. It was from Owen, the kid at Book Soup. He'd searched me out on the store's database to ask about Aeura. A man in a suit came by wanting to meet with him on his break. *Is that cool?* he asked. *Is that normal?* I called back and got an older lady clerk who said Owen was on a break. I saved the voicemail before I ever discovered Owen was missing.

At the after-school debate, I ignored my phone and tried to focus on our team's presentation. VJ was setting up a defense of deed-restricted rent control that destroyed the idea of rent control. He was a conservative and proud of it. Leticia was sitting next to me, and her hand slipped down and clasped mine. At a pause in the action as the Beverly Hills High pro-rent-control debater took a moment to reconfigure his rebuttal, Leticia—never at a lack for confidence—leaned in to whisper in my ear.

Victory party at Starbucks. We got this.

-Patience and preparation.

After-party, you, me, my house. My mother's sunning herself in Costa Rica.

It was setting up like a dream night. My phone was on mute, but it still almost buzzed its way out of my back pocket with a desperate call. I checked the display. It was Aeura calling. I didn't answer. She left a voicemail. As Leticia went to the podium to kill her con argument on a new Constitutional Convention, I listened to the message. It was simple.

Come and get me!

-Damn.

No one heard that. Aeura said she was hiding in the building's loading dock behind a dumpster. There was urgency in her voice and I could tell that she was crying. Was I being played? I blocked it out and concentrated on the debate. Leticia had it all going on.

My topic was next. I gotta tell you, it was not easy putting off Aeura. I knew there was something heinous going down, and she had no part of it. She was as much a victim as her dead stepmother, Delores. Duke always says to trust your gut. Considering his success record it was always a red flag to me as useful advice. I choose to mull over things. My mother was a heady person. She took time and thought things out, at least that's how it seemed to me. Thinking of it now, maybe it was her dealing with life in a second language. When she married Duke after a whirlwind vacation romance in Miami, he moved her permanently to the States. She learned English watching the soaps on TV during the day and working nights as a hostess at Mr. Chow, a block west of Rodeo Drive. I'm sure Duke wooed her promising Beverly Hills, champagne, and caviar. Instead, she got West LA, 5-hour Energy drink, and a Marty's Original hot dog combo. They divorced after two years. She once confessed to me that she never did stop loving him. He never said the same about her. Though he knows it embarrasses me, Duke loves to proclaim he can get laid in five languages. Me, I can't get laid in one. Okay, this is where I admit I am a virgin.

✳ ✳ ✳

Leticia was solid with her Federalist argument peppered with a creationist quote from one of the most obscure and cray cray of the Founding Fathers, Button Gwinnett. Seriously? That reference had the judges dazzled. I took a breath and held back an unstoppable yawn as Beverly Hills High's next debater took the dais. It was Fern Fifer of the Fifer Family Financial Fund fortune. Duke loved to let that trill off his tongue every other week when we did their pool, which lay behind a mansion on one of the more spectacular lots in the coveted flats of the city. A year younger than me, Fern and I have met at least ten times though each time she has no memory of it and asks my name. I am a peon to her and in a way, I enjoy it. Cleaning her pools, I felt invisible. I loved to listen to her inane phone calls with her friends about who had what purse, took what drug, crashed what new car. She's everything I detest, a golden child of generational wealth with that deep breeding sense of entitlement. She was my competition, and I sat up and took in the whole performance.

Fern, to her credit, took a good, long, silent moment to smile at the judges and arrange notes on the lectern. Was I getting squirmy? A little. I mean, you cannot fault the value of her looks, especially since the teachers on the judging panel were both male. She's a notch below model quality. There had been plastic surgery somewhere in her early teens. She's hot and knows it. Is she bright? Maybe. I know she's never had to work hard for anything in her life. And I was proven right. She basically regurgitated word for word the same podcast Leticia had me listen to. She had it down but ran out of steam and neglected to frame it into the con argument. Instead, she kept asking rhetorical questions and stammering under the judges' glare, ill-prepared. The tutor Daddy had no doubt gotten for her would be fired by dinner. Fern helped prove my points, and I knew my rebuttal would obliterate her.

That was all on my mind when I hit the podium with my phone out and toggled Instagram, TikTok, and Facebook for all to see. A little performance art to open my argument and sink Fern's robotic presentation. Everyone, including the judges and the debating teams, has these apps, and I had all of these people where I wanted them. Hypocrites unite! Never too early to log in and gain experience in the virtual fabric of our lives. It was magic. Fern shot me the sneer of death, and I finished to applause. VJ, my toughest critic, gave me a standing *O* and Leticia followed. I went straight for the door. I couldn't stay for the last round with VJ back up to close things out. I had to see what was going on with Aeura for myself. This was not a rash decision. At worst I was on a well-paying job. I hit ACCEPT on the Venmo app and made for the exit to the street.

I was not expecting Leticia to chase me down the steps. She wanted to make sure she'd see me later. I said yes, 'cause you can bet your life that's what I was planning. She kissed me with feeling. On the lips. Ya, right in view of late-leaving students and parents picking them up. It was a nice kiss, an invitation for more. I flew all the way home as if I had wings. Duke was back from the day's jobs and fast asleep in the arms of someone I didn't recognize. I closed the door, grabbed the keys, and took the truck knowing *mi padre* never worked weekends and wouldn't miss it.

There was no way to beat the rush-hour traffic, so I sucked it up like a tourist and hit the 405 North to the San Fernando

Valley. At the first gridlocked dead stop by the Getty, I texted Aeura. It could take a good hour. Could she hold on? She got right back. She had no choice, and this time it was her laying on the emojis with hands clasped in prayer and four yellow danger signs! In a perfectly illegal move that Duke claims to have used in emergencies without getting the $500 ticket, I signaled left and worked my solo self into the swiftly flowing carpool lane, making up time. I only had to go a few miles down the hill to the 134 East, but I was stressed the whole way that I'd get popped by the CHP. Like Duke, I didn't, and I hit the ramp, accelerating toward Burbank and beyond, Glendale.

 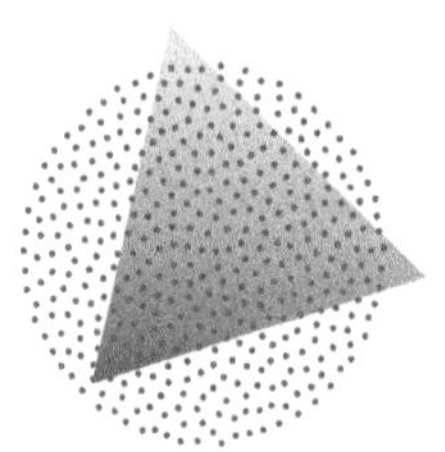

right Now

 Saturday morning's delicious mist is burning off. We are covered with foil blankets and are being treated for our cuts and tears with care inside truck number four, parked in the alley. Couldn't be prouder than to be from the City of Angels and experience these professionals operating. We told the person in charge, Lieutenant Helen Morris, we were runaways sleeping outside for the night and got caught inside. Wrong place, wrong time. And yes, we saw a man pouring gasoline. I think they bought it, though Aeura wears a bracelet that costs more than their yearly salary. Aeura is eating soup in a cup and loving it. We are homeless and surrendering ourselves. I asked Lieutenant Morris to please take us to the station to clean up and she said okay. Mostly because we are now part of an arson investigation. Curious locals and ambulance chasers gawk at us. Beyond them, backlit, I see a dark figure. He's big and wide. I squint hard for a better view, fighting the sun in my eyes. I turn to Aeura.

Do you see that guy? Is that one of them?

-Where?

I look back and he is gone. Aeura turns away. I put a hand on her shoulder, and she shakes it off. Okay. I will give her some space. I want to get back to the fire station and make some calls from their phone. Maybe even to Detective Boylan. Who am I more afraid of? Aeura is wandering off by herself. I want to get her attention. I don't want to use her name.

Hey, girl!

It's called a *withering look*. Aeura can do scorn. At least it got her attention. She admits feeling hopeless. I offer up some plans, argue each on merits, like a debate toss-up. I ask her to stick to the original course of action. Back at Station 77 on a clean phone we can find out what's what. She takes my hand and gives it a squeeze. I feel her gratitude and something more.

16.

friday, yesterday

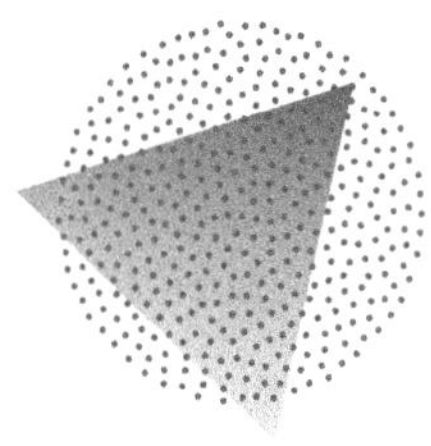

we won the debate.

It didn't hurt to hear what I knew. I was almost in Glendale, passing Hope Drive, which seemed appropriate, when VJ told me the final score. Then he asked me to tighten my seat belt. He had post-debate, breaking news on Leticia. I jumped it.

She cut me from the team for leaving early?

-No, dog. I hate to say this, but she's really into you! I was hoping you'd flame out and give someone else a chance.

You mean like you?

-I wish. Your dreams could come true.

Somehow it didn't feel that way. VJ had also seen the local news covering the Beverly Hills murder. The prime suspect, Sidney Kim, was considered a flight risk as a foreign national and was being held in custody. That made sense. I wondered if Sidney was guilty. I knew Aeura wasn't. Or was she? Did she move the chlorine jug while I was working? She could have. Still, it seemed way unlikely and that kept my foot on the gas straight through to the Glenoaks Boulevard exit. I was working through my thoughts on Aeura, while VJ went on about the news report of the murder. Delores Sung was poisoned, passed out, and hit her head.

Did you hear what I said?

-Yes.

No, you didn't! Delores Sung was poisoned with chlorine. Your chlorine. The jug I packed on the hand truck!

I calmed him down and told him I had already been questioned and was in the clear. That meant he was too. Not to worry. Telling someone not to worry is as effective as telling someone to calm down. Never in the history of calm down has anyone calmed down. VJ was all over me. I admitted I wasn't sure what I was getting into.

Then turn around.

-I can't. I like her. We have this connection.

That is officially the lamest meme.

His phone battery was dying and he had to get off. He threatened to keep calling if I didn't continue to update him. His signal died, sparing me the piling on with more reasons why I was making a mistake. I hooked up my own phone to the charger rigged in the truck and asked Siri to call Duke. If ever I needed some *be in the wind, follow your heart advice,* it was now.

Yo, Gilly the Kid. You okay, partner? You just missed the police.

-*They were at our place?*

Ya, I said I could call you. They said it wasn't necessary. They'd already had you in.

Sure. If you count a parkside chat. Duke seemed unperturbed by the events. He kept saying we dodged a bullet. The Beverly Hills police had searched the apartment and shed. They didn't take anything, and the detective in charge was cool.

He's homegrown. I think we played against each other in Little League.

-*Is this Detective Boylan?*

Uh-huh. He told me we dodged a bullet. You never brought chlorine to Laurel Way. I mean, why would you?

That sounded so wrong I asked him to repeat it. I told him VJ and I did take it and it went missing. He fought that point.

Not missing. Our jug's in the shed. Police saw it.

So that was Boylan's story, and everyone was sticking to it. There was a whole narrative going on that was bogus. I was curious to know more, but Duke had someone at the door. I could hear his Dick Dale, King of the Surf Guitar, "Pipeline" doorbell in the background.

Hold on. Oh, I forgot. The cops did take something you had of that girl's. A book bag with an annotated Virginia Woolf. Knew that wasn't yours. Call you back.

Well, that gave me something to chew on. I negotiated the

Glendale business district, moving slowly up the boulevard. I was close.

Siri, call Book Soup.

The same female worker answered. I inquired again about Owen. This time she could hardly speak.

They found him in La Cienega Park. He's dead.

The steering wheel was shaking under the grip of my spastic hands when the GPS announced with finality, loud and clear, *You have reached your destination.*

It was a low-key, three-story professional building filled with lawyers, doctors, and dentists—Garmenian, Abderian, Hartunian. I wished I was not in such a conspicuous vehicle as Duke's red 1964 Ford Ranchero with its Duke Montrose Pool Service logo emblazoned on the driver and passenger doors. I felt positively naked cruising by. It turned heads on the foggiest day. Glendale was a thriving city at the foot of the San Gabriel Mountains with a big Little Armenia and lots of good, productive citizens, but it was also notorious for its brutal local mob. Why this would be where Aeura was taken is a mystery whose answer I did not want to learn the hard way. I stopped in the alley by the dumpsters, put it in park, and got out. I tossed an old protein bar wrapper of Duke's into the garbage, leaning close, and whispered, *Aeura.*

Without a word, she appeared, hair mussed and rumpled.

Go. Go!

We both got in and I went, went once more. It all felt far too easy. Did they forget about Aeura? From the passenger seat, Aeura looked back and assured me the coast was clear. I figured to get on the freeways to the Westside and head back the same way I came.

Stopped at the traffic light before the on-ramp, Aeura yelled there was a silver Cadillac Escalade following us. To see if she was just being paranoid, I veered for an In-N-Out on the corner and got in the drive-thru lane of our cherished LA burger chain. The silver SUV did not follow and went on its way. We were relieved enough to order a couple of "animal-style" burgers, fries, and shakes. With the awesome takeout we drove surface streets out of Glendale up to a Burbank park in the shadow of the 134 and parked on a side street. We ate our dinner in silence, in the dark, savoring every bite. When we finished, she filled me in as best as she could. She was being pressured by the lawyers to sign a statement against her father. If she didn't, she could be charged as an accomplice.

Even my mother thinks he's guilty. And she wonders about me!

Aeura's mother might be in line for a rich piece of the IPO, and like all the partners she had an eye on that prize. Delores Sung's considerable share now would go to Sidney Kim. This salient point the police had seized on as the motive. Of course, if Kim was convicted, it could be forfeited, no? Were we the only ones seeing this? We cleaned up after ourselves and tossed the empty bags in the trash. Back in the car I asked her the most pressing question.

Where can you go?

-I was hoping you may have a thought.

I had nothing. My phone buzzed with a text tone, saving me the embarrassment. It was VJ typing away. The Beverly

Hills police had just visited him, getting their chlorine story straight. Boylan? Of course. The bullshit was so transparent. I had heard Duke rant on about Beverly Hills and its cover-up of famous solved and unsolved crimes. Listen, every time we passed Whittier Drive on Sunset he would go on about the murder of Ronni Chasen, a Hollywood PR maven, which the police pinned on some random homeless guy on a bike. When the rando was found a day later, he panicked and shot himself in front of the city cops. The case was closed even though no one believed it was the guy or the gun. Someone had gotten away with murder. SOP in BH.

Aeura tapped my hand to get my attention.

What is your friend saying?

-Basically—your father is being set up.

I was telling her something she already knew. There were forces at work and they were stacked against her. I offered up the idea she could go to the airport and fly home. I could cover it with my debit card. She gave the sweetest, saddest smile. She had no makeup on after being held at the office, and I could really see her. I focused on Aeura's features, which were unlike any girl I'd known. Her eyes were obsidian almonds, radiant and grateful. Her skin, oh her skin. I did not understand why she hid under the dark goth filter. She was an Asian in America. Was she ashamed? Her mouth, the smallest, most perfect oval formed my name.

Gilly, I can't even leave the county, according to the lawyer.

-So...back to Laurel Way?

Before she could reject that option, we saw a massive figure crossing the street—walking hard, right for us. I started up the truck, put it in drive, and then hit the brake a split second after. The silver Escalade had come out of nowhere and T-boned the space in front, blocking our way forward. The looming figure striding for us we recognized. He was security guard #1, Hartunian, from Laurel Way—the beefy hulk (is that redundant?)! He pulled out a gun. Aeura screamed.

Go! Go!

Twitch! I went, went and banged the truck in reverse. I did not expect him to shoot at us! Bullets shattered the side panel glass. Oh, Duke, please forgive! Accelerating backward, I missed a parking meter and the Ranchero's back wheels caught the edge of the curb. Onto the sidewalk we went. Our heads low, I kept it in reverse, driving backward, straight onto the grass of the empty (thank God) park. I spun out on the wet turf, and the trusty truck lurched forward, rumbling across a Little League diamond's outfield and an open accessway to a street on the park's other side.

We were lucky and got to Riverside Drive before Aeura saw the Escalade a few cars behind us. I went with what I knew and sped north. Duke's truck may look vintage, but it has a V-8 with 326 horses and Duke brags it can still take on Corvettes. I was headed for San Fernando Boulevard, a broad, broken asphalt roadway in nearby Sun Valley. It was a forgotten oasis of junkyards where Duke and I spent many a weekend buying and selling and hanging out playing cards. We ditched the Ranchero on the roadside, and Aeura helped me cover it with fallen palm fronds that littered the way.

There was no time to get it perfect. We ran for a yard I knew and crawled under the fence through a hole that party crashers, including me, had dug to get into Duke's junkyard bachelor bash. After a few tries, stumbling in the dark, I found the enormous, pink-painted, steel propane tank from the party and we climbed inside and hid.

That was yesterday. Hopefully we will survive today. This recording is over.

Leticia

right Now

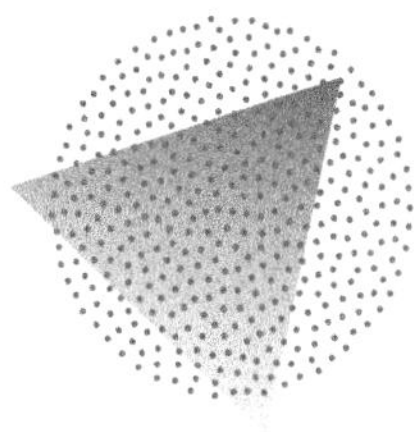

for the first time since i picked up Aeura in gLeNdALe, MY stoMACH is Not tied iN kNots. We are safe at Station 77. I love LA. I am eating the most delicious roach-coach breakfast burrito and washing it down with superpowered fire station coffee. The morning sun is burning off the low-hanging valley mist, and it's already warm for a winter morning.

Saturday morning. I should be sleeping in. Duke will be. I dread calling him. The abandoned Ranchero truck may or may not have been found by those f'ers. I am giving it till ten o'clock and a chance to have dear old dad awake. I have not been able to speak to VJ yet. He is not answering his phone. I have been charging mine with the help of the station charger and will turn it on to check for messages soon. Aeura has not turned on her charged-up phone. We don't know if the phones are being monitored and will give us away. Or how high up this cover-up goes. How could they be so brazen, so confident that they won't be caught? So *bulletproof,* as Duke is known to say. I know Aeura wants to speak to her father. How to do that is another question. From what VJ said, he's being held in the Beverly Hills jail till he is arraigned. That could be Monday, an eternity away.

Aeura, is there anyone you can call to get a message to him?
-Not that I trust.
Okay. Let me call Duke.

I power up my phone and see a notification from one and the same.

GET LOST! DON'T CALL ME. I AM SERIOUS.

Scratch that idea. And there was also a text from VJ.

DON'T REPLY. EVERYBODY IS AFTER YOU AND THAT KOREAN GIRL. STAY SAFE.

Got it. Thanks, bro. The expiration date for staying safe seems to have passed. We cannot stay at the station. We need to go somewhere back on the Westside where no one will find us. It's a reach but I have a crazy notion. I pull up the Uber app on my phone and tap in the Westwood address on Montana Avenue that Leticia had sent me.

ʃaturday

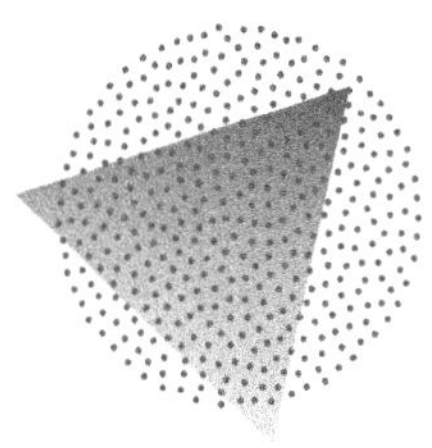

with her ʃinɡle mom off in coʃtA ricA, Leticia, still in her bathrobe and slippers, had been bingeing a streaming historical drama for school credit when the doorbell chimed. She opened the double oaken portals of the fine house south of Wilshire in the shadow of the Mormon Temple and let us in. It was awkward, yes. She was confused. Aeura was too. The moment I introduced them to each other, I could see each wondered whether the other was in a relationship with me. I mean, talk about being flattered. If only... I didn't waste words.

I asked Leticia if we could hang out for a few hours until I could negotiate a surrender to the authorities.

And this is because why?

-Because people are trying to kill us.

Gilly, can we talk in private?

I followed her into the kitchen. She turned on the sink to mask our conversation.

Is this a prank?

-Would that be better?

Better than what?

-The truth? Aeura's father is being framed for a murder in Beverly Hills.

Leticia took it well and looked me in the eye and wondered.

Do you still want to go out with me?

-Huh? Is that a condition for us staying?

What?

-I mean, of course I want to.

Leticia brightened, turned off the faucet, and removed her glasses. The five-star goddess I have hungered for, joined the debate team for, and dreamed about took me in her arms and planted an intense kiss on my lips. Either I was dehydrated or I was really seeing stars. The day was exploding with wonderful possibilities. The kiss was going off in stages like a SpaceX rocket—when there was a scream from the living room.

Aeura had collapsed in a fetal heap on the sofa, pointing at the TV. *Breaking News* bannered on a newsbreak crawl with footage.

That's my father!

Leticia unmuted the sound, and the on-air reporter's words iced the room. While in custody, the suspect accused of the Jacuzzi Murder in Beverly Hills had committed suicide. He'd hanged himself in the cell. Aeura quaked with a moaning sound from a deep well of sorrow we could only imagine. Leticia and I sat down and held her, giving all the warmth and solace we had.

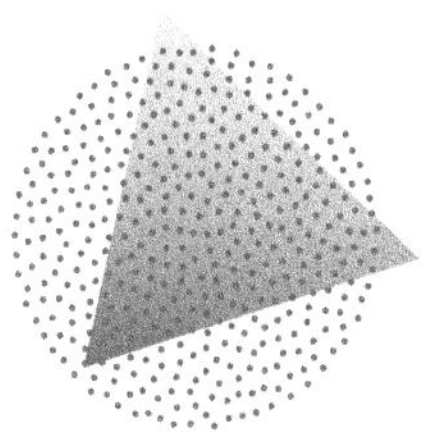

3.

right now

Aeura wants to go the police station, and I can't think of a reason to stop her. The guilt or innocence of her dad seems irrelevant. We are hoping she and I are no longer seen as a threat. Is this wishful thinking? Leticia is helping. It means a lot to me. We are in Leticia's mother's BMW SUV. Leticia will go into the police station first, without us. Sitting behind Leticia in the back seat, I am not surprised her hands are "10–2" on the steering wheel, textbook correct. That's how she rolls. Westwood to Beverly Hills is not a long ride.

Aeura sits next to Leticia in the front seat. My crammed tall frame stretches out. I can't ignore Leticia moving her right hand from the wheel and clasping Aeura's left as she drives. Aeura's plight has become a crusade, and Leticia is a force for good. I wonder about the gangsters who tried to kill us. Had Sidney Kim's partners hired them? Could they call off the dogs now that he is dead? Or are the partners not the ones behind this plot? And Detective Boylan? I'm not sure where he stands. Duke told me in all caps to **GET LOST**. I haven't. Just the opposite. Is it up to Aeura and me to expose the killers of a case the police have already closed?

At the Beverly Hills City Hall center, anchored by the most incredible gilded-domed, art deco building, with a seven-story, mission bell tower, I go all tour guide for Aeura's benefit. Leticia, who is smarter than me, adds that the historic edifice represents the California churrigueresque style. She parks by the police station in a blue-lined accessible spot up front by the amazing gardens. Her mother, Bethany Almora, is a divorcée, single mom, and UCLA professor with a knee replacement and a placard for her tennis injury. I assure Letica that I will move the car if there is a problem. Before she heads off on our fact-finding mission with the police, Leticia braces Aeura and tells her not to worry. They hug, and then they pull me into the embrace. This feels wildly good. I have underestimated Leticia's ability to empathize.

Leticia gets out and I move up to the driver's seat. Aeura and I relax and power up the beemer, rolling down the windows. A jasmine-scented breeze drifts through. Before I can identify for Aeura the source of the scent, a silver Cadillac SUV pulls into the spot next to us. Two men get out. The one from the passenger door, a beast in a tight suit, I recognize as the damn gate guard, Hartunian, from Laurel Way! I can't sink into my seat fast enough. He is looking right at me and Aeura, who is in shock. I do not hesitate. The car roars to life. I hit reverse and jam on the accelerator. Aeura, unbelted, nearly hits the windshield. I squeal into a skid and swerve around, executing a perfect donut. All my practice as a student driver playing skid marks in the library parking lot with VJ is paying off. We are away. Aeura does not see them following.

You sure?

-Gilly, he waved goodbye!

What?!

We fire up Burton Way and head south out of the city. At Olympic Boulevard I make a right and slide into traffic on the broad causeway headed for Santa Monica and the beach. I glance over at Aeura with a shrug.

I did tell Leticia I'd move the car if there was a problem.

4.

saturday

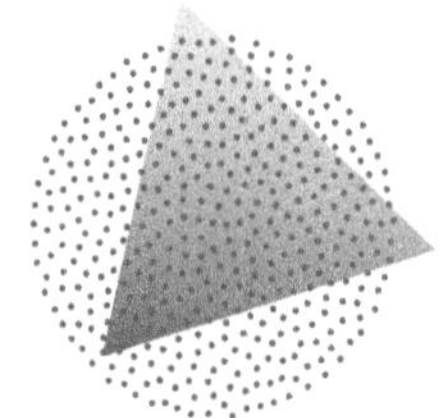

i had taken aeura to the venice fishing pier as a safe harbor until we knew more. I admit I was not taking any chances. North of the pier it's *locals only* surfing, and one of the old, wet-suited men coming out of the water I recognized as Chuck, a friend of Duke's. He let me use his cell so that I didn't have to use mine. While Chuck flamed up a doobie the size of a Cuban cigar, I was able to safely text Leticia. She texted back with angry emojis about her mother's car but got the picture. She hailed an Uber west to catch up with us at the head of the long pier. I wasn't sure if it was the allure and excitement of our true crime plight or if Leticia was making sure Aeura didn't have an unfair advantage with me.

Sitting out in the early afternoon sun, it was a perfect LA day. Fishermen, mostly Mexican, baited, cast, and occasionally hit pay dirt and reeled in some dinner. It was sweet. And life-affirming, compared to Leticia relaying her experience. She'd gone to the main desk and said she had information about the "Jacuzzi Murder case," as the news media had labeled it. After a runaround, she was handed off to a Detective Boylan who told her we were no longer *persons of interest*. He cut it short to meet up with a swarthy man in a too-tight suit. When I described his features, she confirmed Aeura's and my worst fear. The Glendale gang and Boylan were allied in this business. The best takeaway, according to Leticia, was that they no longer seemed to be after us. We asked Aeura again if her father could have killed his wife. Leticia, ever the cause-and-effect explorer, couldn't help herself.

I mean, why else did he kill himself?

-He did not kill himself!!!

Aeura screamed that, and the fishermen and tourists took notice. I tried to lower the temperature.

Aeura, we are just spinning scenarios.

-No harm, no foul.

--My father is dead! Leave me alone!

Pissed and irrational, she walked away from us down the pier toward Washington Boulevard and into the Venice street scene. I got up to go after her. Leticia stopped me.

She'll be back. She has nowhere else to go.

Leticia tugged at me and I sat down. Aeura did not return.

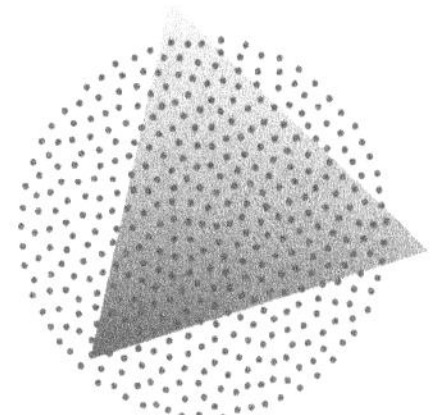

5.

rigHt Now

it feeLs Like it's over. it feeLs Like it's begiNNiNg.
I am at Leticia's house spooning with her on her living room
couch, and it feels so right. It's been an exhausting few days,
and this feeling of unabated leisure feels positively stolen.
There's a song Duke likes that describes it: "Afternoon Delight."
That feeling. I know it can't last. Especially with Leticia surfing
the web on her iPad while I hold her in my arms.

There! Here it is. I knew it had to have happened.

She hits play. We watch a video of a news conference from

Beverly Hills on the Jacuzzi Murder case. It is the Beverly Hills district attorney. He goes on and on, saying little. Domestic murder-suicide of foreign nationals, blah, blah, blah. He does say they are no longer looking for suspects. Sidney Kim murdered his wife and then hanged himself. The Korean authorities reached the same conclusion. The case is closed, blah, blah, blah. I am relieved when she stops the video. Leticia is hot. Not in a good way.

Fake news. You don't buy that, do you?

-Of course not. But what can we do?

What about the clerk at Book Soup? You said he was murdered. Why?

I have no quick answer for her. I am bursting into the denim of my jeans, and she sees it. My face is red.

Get a grip, Gilly. VJ is coming. He's done some background work for us.

-What?!

Refocus! Do we need to go to Book Soup?

The doorbell rings, and the door opens. VJ is all smiles joining us!

Hey, fugitives! The heat is off. Where's Aeura Kim?

He looks around and Leticia and I stare blankly. Good question. Both Leticia's and my cell phones erupt. Question answered. It's Aeura!

saturday

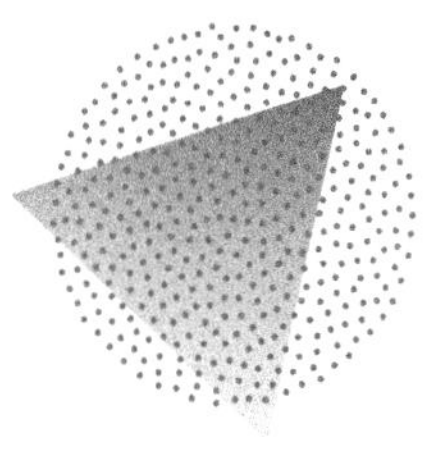

 Aeura had taken a Lyft from Venice to Laurel Way. Her mother wanted her home. She was convinced Aeura's father had done a terrible thing. Two terrible things. He'd sent Aeura's mother—his ex-wife and college sweetheart—an email from a business account explaining it. She'd turned it over to the Beverly Hills investigator in charge.

He could not live with himself.

She begged Aeura to listen. And for once Aeura intended

to and was planning to take the evening flight her mom had booked. At Laurel Way, the oblivious K-pop girls were at the pool counting TikTok views and giggling at their cleverness. While Aeura packed up her things in the guest bedroom, she checked out their TikTok page on her phone. There was Gilly's butt crack swaying—as predicted—to a "Gangnam Style" song. The video went on repeat, and this time something in the background could not be unseen.

Aeura called us to see for ourselves on TikTok.

Search @2hyunghyung and watch.

VJ had it up on his cell before any of us.

Got it! Oh cool. Gill man's vertical smile!

-Freeze at twenty-four seconds and enlarge.

Oh shit! I told you I packed the chlorine!

VJ froze the frame image. I did, too, and enlarged it. There was no mistaking what she'd discovered. The security guard, Hartunian, is unmistakable—on camera—removing from our hand truck the old black milk crate with a big jug of chlorine.

right now

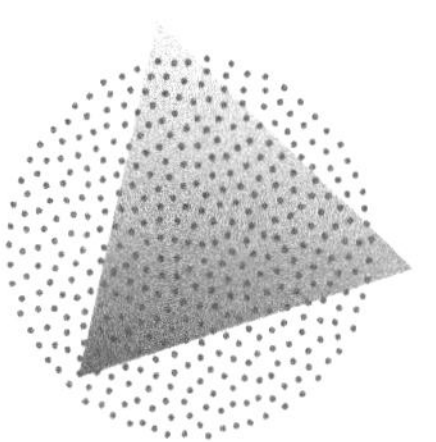

Aeura joins us in a parking lot across from La Cienega park on the west Hollywood side. She is not going back to Houston tonight. She gets in the back seat where VJ is distributing to Leticia and me stellar takeout from Le Pho WeHo that he got Postmates to deliver to our car—I mean, Leticia's mom's car. Aeura gets a Styrofoam cup brimming with heavenly pho broth, noodles, and veggie goodies. It's a big hit with Aeura, whose newly applied eye makeup runs from the steam and emotion. It makes her look more goth than usual.

We take the time to nourish and get acquainted.

Aeura, that slick dude is VJ.

-Ah yes. Our outside man.

VJ, Aeura Kim.

--The most innocent daughter. Pleased to meet you.

---He's been looking into the company's IPO prospectus.

Leticia, as always, is on point. Aeura brightens with gratitude and gives VJ a fetching smile. VJ, who has that aversion to Koreans (or so he says) looked very comfortable sharing the seat with a young Korean female. Leticia—bless her heart—presses on with VJ in support.

It would be good to establish a motive.

-Aeura, did your father ever talk about his partners? This James Hyung and Rodney Allan?

--He wanted them to buy him out before it went public. His wife, Delores, wouldn't let him.

---She was the biggest investor.

VJ has the data. Aeura takes a moment and cries without restraint.

He was so mad at her. Maybe he did kill her! Then killed himself. I'm sorry!

-Well, score one for the BHPD. Even a blind squirrel... Hey, spring rolls are still warm.

--Hold on! What about the dead bookseller?

----And the chlorine jug cover-up?

--And Armenian gangsters trying to burn us alive?

Aeura does not have to be reminded of that. She can smell our singed hair. There are too many loose ends, and we all know it. So why don't the police? It seems as good a time as any to replay the voicemail from Owen and share its implications.

Finish chewing and listen.

VJ crunches his spring roll through the final bite, and I hit play.

Hey, Guillermo. This is Owen, not a stalker. I found your number in our store's VIP customer database. A man wants to meet on my lunch hour. Is this normal before going out with Aeura? Please call back.

The silence in the car was profound. I confess to all with sudden, unquenchable regret that I didn't get the message in time. My phone was turned off when I was with Detective Boylan.

He never came back from his lunch hour.

-What's the status of this investigation?

--Probably over.

VJ has done his homework, and on the mobile Citizen app he saw a 2:02 p.m. post that reported the BHPD had arrested a suspect in the La Cienega Park murder. A homeless guy on a bike, a robbery gone wrong. The comments that followed on the app were a flurry of thoughts and prayers, similar stories about robbery attempts by the unhoused, and righteous outrage that the city is no longer safe. Are we the only ones who see what a load of crap that is? Does anyone want to know what this is really about? Homeless guy on a bike? Is that their go-to cover-up? My cell rings and it's Duke.

You'll never guess where I am.

-Can I wish instead? Sun Valley?

You owe me, kid. Luckily I have free glass replacement insurance.
-How did you get out there?
A special friend. Don't count on me for dinner.
-Nice.

Dad is surprised I am not more upbeat. He was notified by Detective Boylan that we were in the clear. He also spoke to his pal, the homeowner, who is happy to say the Korean renter and his family are cool with everything and still in residence.

This James Hyung is a good guy. Didn't ask for any money back. My advice, forget everything that happened.
-That is not going to be easy.

Before he gets off the call, Duke tries to be fatherly and help me through my trauma. He only understands sex, drugs, and rock and roll and suggests any or all three for a remedy.

Or go to that bookstore you love. Feed your head.
-Thanks, Dad.
What? No? You think it's the old Beverly Hills bamboozle?
-Ya, Dad. I do.

Duke doesn't respond at first. I think the call is over. It is not.

You want to get to the truth?
-Ya. You offering directions?
Better.

I know this will be priceless and put the Dukester on speaker so my car mates can appreciate what I put up with. Duke delivers.

Expect a call from Abby Jo Feinstein. You remember her?

I do. Insane, alcoholic, shit disturber. Before I can yell NO! he hangs up. I explain to everyone that Abby Jo is an old high-school GF of Duke's who has been a reporter for the *LA Weekly* for a zillion years—a total conspiracy nut, chain-smoking communist, born too late to be a '60s revolutionary.

He can't be serious. Duke refers to her as Ms. Buttinsky. Not a compliment.

-She's an investigative journalist? That could help, no?

Leticia sees value. No. I don't want to encourage this. My last experience with Abby Jo was coming home from the library and seeing her heave heavy objects at Duke over his failure to vote in a local election.

It's nothing. She's a whack job. She will not call.

That creates an awkward silence in the car, a hopelessness, a letdown. Aeura fades back into her seat, energy ebbing. Leticia sinks down into her private thoughts. VJ scrounges for another morsel of takeout. I am thinking about putting on a soothing Ed Sheeran ditty to ease the pain—when my phone chimes. Leticia is on me like a cat, poking, prodding.

Answer it!

I do and hit my phone's speaker button. I greet Abby Jo with my most polite enthusiasm. Not that manners matter to her. She cuts me off with a voice like splintered wood.

--He didn't do it.

That gets everyone's attention.

ſaturday

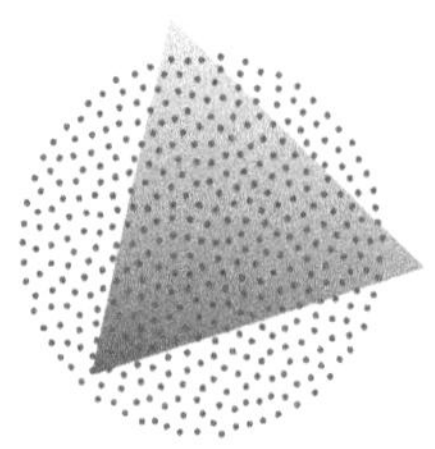

WE MET ABBY JO FEINſTEIN AT HER ONE-ROOM APARTMENT hidden within the legendary Los Altos Apartments, mid-city Wilshire, a throwback mission-style apartment complex with a crazy Hollywood history. It was once a classic fortress for the wild and creative. Now it's all trendy, mega-priced units for those not on rent control for thirty years like Abby Jo. She asked us to park two blocks away, come up one at a time, in one-minute intervals, and to make sure we weren't followed. She also asked that we bring a bottle of Tito's vodka, a pack of Marlboro Lights, and a bag of Cape Cod sea salt and vinegar potato chips.

We each navigated through a rabbit warren series of hallways and stairs to a secret floor once used by Clara Bow to meet her lover. Clara was the Taylor Swift of her time. A silent film actress who captivated the globe with her distinctive haircut and sexy allure. Abby Jo's high gray afro was the first thing you noticed about her. She was Duke's age and wore an African dashiki. Her place felt like a den of '70s relics and journalism awards, which it was. As a professional Abby Jo had burned all her bridges to light her erratic way and never achieved the career she could have had, sayeth the Duke. She also was quite a beauty in her day. Not so much anymore. In the harsh overhead light, time and bad habits had ravaged her face into a bitter question mark of anxiety and—dare I say—paranoia. She waited till the four of us were all in, double-locked the door, relit a cigarette butt, and then laid it on us.

Something stinks!

She told us she had a hair up her ass for city hall corruption. Beverly Hills elite-on-elite crime got her panties in a twist, she spit out. It was a lot of information we didn't care about, but then she showed us what had irked her.

I have a friend at police headquarters whom I blackmail occasionally. She got me the witness statements from when Delores Sung's—the wife's—body was first discovered.

With blue surgical gloves Abby Jo held up her iPad for each of us. She asked that we identify ourselves, swear to not reveal the source of the information, and to read on.

Don't touch please. Just use your eyes and you'll see how lame. They couldn't get their stories straight. A security guard—Rob Hartunian—and Korean James Hyung who started his professional career back in Hong Kong. They both say the daughter was with the father. A housekeeper, Estella Franco, says the daughter ran off before and was gone. You're the daughter?

Aeura nodded. I told Abby Jo that Aeura was with me when I left the property. And when I split, the victim was alive. Leticia tried to catch her up on more of our discovery.

There also was the murder of a bookstore clerk who would have confirmed the housekeeper's version. Are we certain she's still alive?

Abby Jo cracked open the Tito's and took a slug out of the vodka bottle. She literally gargled with it before swallowing, didn't say a word, and left the apartment. I felt like I had wasted everyone's time for an uncomfortable five minutes till Abby Jo returned and threw down a thick, dusty file.

Cui bono. The Armenian mob and the Beverly Hills Police Department have been in and out of bed for a while. Why? I don't know, but we are going to find out.

With excitement, Leticia squeezed my right hand, Aeura my left. VJ announced what we all were thinking.

We follow the money!

Abby Jo corrected him.

No. We follow the sex!

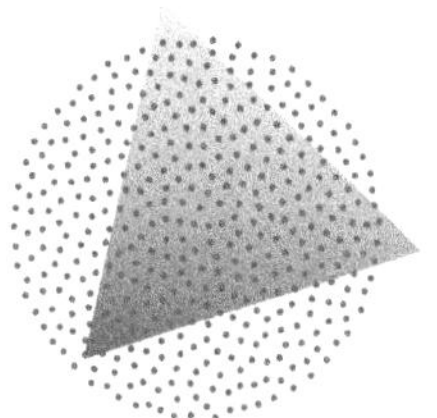

right Now

Cozying up in the back seat are Leticia and VJ, who have Aeura sandwiched in the middle. I am at the wheel. Abby Jo is my navigator, riding shotgun and eating potato chips. We are off in pursuit of a sex worker confidante of Abby Jo's. It's Saturday night, and I am trying to resist the urge to put some dancing music on. Sweet relief pours out of every pore of my skin. The length of the drive has diluted the passion of the mission. We are safe. Life is normal. Even Aeura has lightened up and laughs at something I can't hear over Abby Jo's loud munching. The release after running for my life is making me loopy. From the girls' giggling in the back seat, I can tell VJ is making smooth moves with the ladies. Duke calls it, *Full of young, dumb, and rhymes with plum.* Only Abby Jo has her jaw set tight. I try to remember something but can't. That feeling in your stomach when nothing is all you can come up with. I think it's a good thing. I drive on and silently celebrate wondering if I had a choice between Aeura and Leticia whom I might choose. Duke always says there will be days like this. Days you want to tell everyone what it feels like to be fancy free with no hellhound on your tail. Abby Jo coughs, choking on a chip, and raises a hand to say she's all right.

Christina will have heard something. If we're lucky she'll let you all come inside the house. It's early for her, and she likes to look at young, pretty people.

-Oh really? That's cool.

It helps the imagination later when you have a 250-pound, hairy gangster using you as a blow-up toy. So is your father dating anyone?

I want to say everyone, but out of respect for Abby Jo I say he's pretty involved with one.

Someone age appropriate? Don't answer that.

-Thanks.

He could really light up a cold night. Sorry. Make a right on Barham.

I follow Abby Jo's directions up into the mouth of a Burbank canyon and up a hilly ridge road. The rain that was predicted to be extreme at times is making the forecasters look good.

Heavy drops have started tattooing the roof and windshield. We stop in front of a cute, ivy-covered Craftsman. I look for a place to park on the narrow, winding lane. My car-ma hits jackpot. A black Tesla is pulling out of a prime spot across from the cottage. My headlights wash over the vehicle as it heads away. Aeura IDs the driver before Abby Jo recognizes him.

It's Mr. Allan, one of my father's partners.

-Rodney Allan. Ex-con, Beverly Hills bottom-feeder.

My foot is in spasms, tapping the accelerator, with something like unbridled fear invading my flesh and bones. The Tesla tail-lights vanish in my rearview mirror. This cannot be a coincidence. This is all wrong. No one says anything. After a fierce swig of Tito's, Abby Jo lights a Marlboro Light.

Now we're having fun.

10.

ſaturday Night

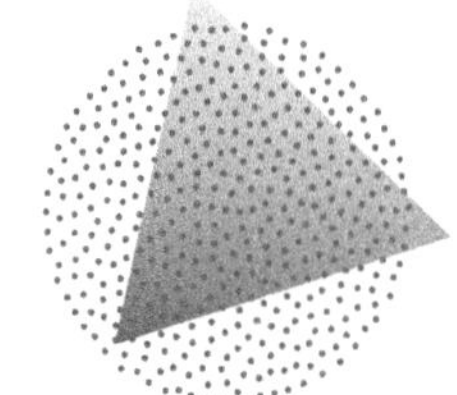

ABBY JO TOLD US TO WAIT IN THE CAR for her while she moved up the path to the cottage alone. We were not the only ones watching her. We saw her enter through the vine-covered portico, imagining the direst scenarios. If all our TV-watching taught us nothing else, the consensus among us was that Abby Jo would soon be screaming at the sight of her dead friend silenced forever by Rodney Allan. We listened but no scream ensued. Nothing stirred from the house. The rain picked up. We waited and waited, and Abby Jo did not reappear. It was

VJ who insisted we investigate after a good five minutes had passed. For safety's sake, I second-guessed it.

A little more time won't kill us.

-Bad choice of words. I'm with VJ.

Leticia got out of the car with him. They were mere steps up the path to the cottage when Aeura and I sprang forth from the car to join, all wet. I was trying to be the adult and not put us in danger, but the peer pressure, you know? We amassed at the wrought-iron and wood front door under a much-needed porch roof, uncertain how to proceed. Leticia knocked with urgency. No response. With the gentlest touch, I turned the knob. The door swung open to an unoccupied, brightly decorated living room. A plush leopard-skin couch and cowhide chairs surrounded a baroque-as-hell, marble-topped coffee table. On it were a couple of shot glasses and highballs, one with a vodka shot still in it. Smoke drifted from a cigarette left burning in a vintage ceramic ashtray with a pinup girl painted in the center. Leticia whispered.

Marlboro Lights. It's Abby Jo's. She's here.

I went for it and called out her name with the ferocity of a rescue rope. No one called back. The adjoining kitchen had been recently used, and dishes were in the sink.

-Abby Jo!

Leticia went down the hallway, poking around.

Anyone here?

Only silence. It was eerie quiet. Aeura felt a shiver and found comfort in VJ's arms. I was sure it was because he was closest to her. I followed Leticia. She opened another door. This one led to a bedroom. If any Hollywood art director was looking to design and dress a pro's boudoir, they could use this for authenticity and inspiration. There were oriental carpets, silk shawls tossed everywhere, painted parasols hanging from the ceiling, and a Tiffany disco ball. The walls were covered with artful, antique oil paintings of seminude beauties in classical poses. The open armoire with an array of sex toys on the shelves was perfect. The bed was recently—perhaps professionally—used. The only thing out of place was a small pearl-handled revolver lying on a pillow. Leticia gasped and I steadied her in my arms. She relaxed and patted my shoulder with a sweet touch.

Everyone agreed not to touch the gun, which could be evidence. Aeura put a hand close and said it had not been fired. VJ confirmed it.

We didn't panic but searched the other, smaller bedroom. It was empty and appeared unused. I peeked under the California King bedsprings to double-check and was relieved to find only a sleeping black cat.

Ow!

Claws out, the cat was not sleeping. I stood up, and Aeura checked my hand with a tenderness I had not expected.

No blood.

-Thanks.

--C'mon! He's fine.

Did I detect some jealousy? Leticia made a swift exit and rounded a corner that led to a rear door. It was wide open to the elements. The overhead light was out, and the darkness revealed little of the hilly terrain beyond a service porch that abutted a near-vertical backyard. We used our phones' flashlights to see into the woodsy abyss and could only make out a woodsier abyss. Back in the cottage we all agreed that while we were waiting in the car, we saw no one exit or enter the house from the front. The rear exit seemed limited to traversing up the steep hillside to nowhere. Could there be another way? Aeura and I tripped over each other with the most obvious answer. VJ right behind us.

Like a basement?

-There has to be one!

--Or a secret passageway to a secret room.

---A classy dungeon. The kind S&M clients appreciate. Don't ask how I know this.

We did not ask Leticia, as requested, though I made a note to myself to find out sometime. I mean, wouldn't you?

Look for a trap door.

--Or a loose panel.

VJ and I were on it before Leticia said it. We rolled up every rug we could find in the living areas and found nothing. Aeura and Leticia felt along all the walls and got the same nothing. We went back to the first bedroom. I moved some toys on a shelf to feel behind, and one of them snapped back into its place. It was a lever disguised as a long, slightly curved dildo. As the others watched with encouragement, I reached for it.

VJ! Do not say a word.

He didn't, but I felt a rush of embarrassment before the lovelies just the same. There seemed only one way to do this. I grabbed the dildo and pushed it down hard. A creak groaned, building like something out of a horror movie or a Scooby-Doo cartoon. The armoire slid over to reveal a passageway. All talking stopped as we considered the next step. Aeura took the initiative.

I'll go first.

VJ and I were not about to let that happen and mounted a vigorous defense. In response Aeura picked up the gun from the pillow.

Don't worry, I'm from Texas. I know how to use it. And…it's my mother's.

That hit like a brick. She showed off the revolver's handle. Inset into the white pearl were black obsidian initials, *T.K.*

Tomoko Kim.

Aeura spun the cylinder to check for bullets and snapped it back into place with a pro move. Locked and loaded. Out of respect and caution we gave her a wide berth. She stepped forward and went first into the passageway.

12.

right NOW

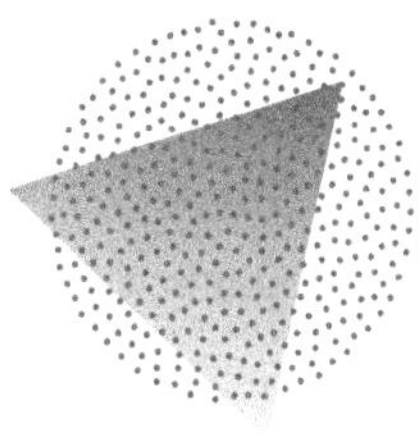

i AM the LAſt iN. The secret hallway leads to a stone-lined room at the end, with an open door. There is no one inside. It is a modern dungeon bathed in a red overhead light. The most prominent piece is a big padded wooden chair with restraints on the armrests and legs. There are also two small tiltable tables with access holes and furry restraints. On one wall are whips of various sizes and styles, face cages, studded leather masks, and other hand tools to deliver pain. Feathers and oils to deliver pleasure are stacked on an overhead shelf. It's more hard-core than classy.

I am way creeped out. People enjoy this?

VJ says what I am thinking, and I am glad it is him. Leticia sits in the chair.

Did you not see Fifty Shades of Grey? Kink has its fans.

--Ah. Like...you?

What? Gilly, don't go all pervo on me!

I am so sorry I took the bait. VJ laughs. Aeura tucks the gun away.

Where is Abby Jo? Or anyone? How could she disappear?

No one has an answer. We sit on the tables' edges facing one another and ponder. I have to ask.

Aeura, your mother's gun—how did it end up here?

Aeura wants to answer that. We all want her to and hang on every bit of her body language as she begins to muster up a possible explanation. I hear something outside the room and turn. It is too late. The door to the dungeon slams shut with us inside. We rush to the door and can hear the bolt outside bang into place. Locked!

No!

-Help!

--Damn!

---Screw you!

It erupts from Aeura—the grief, frustration, and anger, followed by the sound of that pearl-handled revolver blasting bullets into the wooden door. We all cower as she lets loose. I count the discharges at six, and though she keeps squeezing the trigger the chambers are spent. We all rise and push that door with all our collective might. It does no good. The door's iron bolt holds. We all know Aeura's wasted the ammo. Her mother's gun is no longer of use for our defense. I hold Aeura from behind, steadying her. She quakes under my touch. Leticia reaches for me in this dark moment and holds me and Aeura in her arms. Not one to be a fourth wheel, VJ piles on to our group hug of togetherness and love.

We are on a double date from hell, trapped in an escape room without any clues.

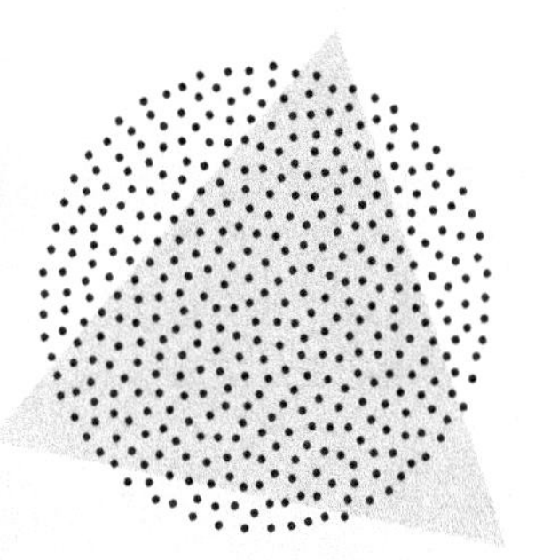

8.

saturday, earlier

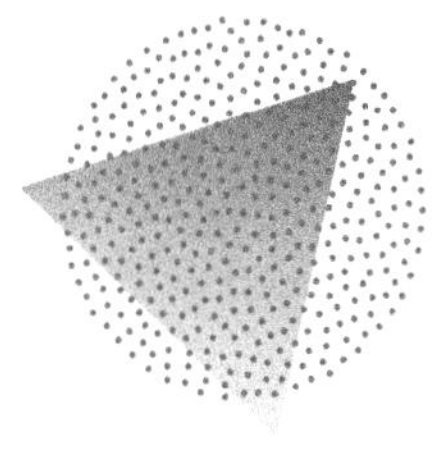

TOMOKO KIM FLEW IN FROM HOUSTON WHEN HER DAUGHTER DID NOT FLY BACK AS ARRANGED. The fifty-year-old, Seoul-born divorcée let concern and general bitterness drive her. She took a cab from the airport to the Laurel Way house to confront her ex-husband's partners and to protect her and her daughter's share of the IPO. James Hyung was there to greet her. A lifetime ago they were more than friends, and Tomoko felt safe with the familiar face. Hyung insisted she stay with them as long as she needed. Tomoko appreciated the generosity. She knew Hyung's wife, who had remained back in Asia to mother their ten-year-old. Tomoko had no intention of trying to sweet-talk Hyung, though she knew what turned him on.

She did not feel the same comfort level with the American partner, Rodney Allan. She had heard from her late ex that Allan was dishonorable, and with that foreknowledge she kept distant as they met by the pool. James was surprised to learn that Aeura had disappeared and felt concern for her safety. That was not comforting news to Tomoko. The best hold she had on any of the multibillion IPO jackpot was through her daughter. With Sidney and his wife now deceased, Tomoko believed their share now went to Aeura and a smaller share to her from the divorce settlement. Allan assured her she was mistaken. The circumstances of the murder and suicide disqualified the disbursement, according to their lawyers.

It will be forfeited back to the company.

Tomoko had lawyers, too, and a lot to say, but it was not the time and place. Like a good, old-world Korean, she demurred, lowered her head, and excused herself.

A new housekeeper, replacement for Estela Franco who had left the country on a family emergency, showed Tomoko to a guest suite in the Beverly Hills mansion. Before she entered, Tomoko caught sight of James Hyung's two teen daughters and warmly waved. They were in pajamas though it was midday. They pretended not to recognize Tomoko and disappeared down the hall. Had they been coached to avoid her? It made Aeura's mother more determined than ever to renegotiate a fair share with Hyung. Before she could unpack there was a friendly knock on the door. Surprised, she admitted James Hyung.

Let me start over. I'm terribly sorry about Sidney and Delores.

-I appreciate that.

Hyung was days away from becoming insanely rich and had never felt more stressed. He sat on the bed and stressed to Tomoko that he had invented the idea for their humble start-up, the Crypto Mining League. Sidney Kim, his dear friend from university in Seoul, had provided the necessary original mathematical algorithmic solutions, but the genius and credit was Hyung's. Even Rodney Allan, who provided the capital, knew this IPO would not be possible without Hyung's brilliance in creating crypto as sport with competitive, professional digital-mining teams. It had never been done, and Wall Street was salivating over the bitcoin profit generated. Despite all the negativity caused by the Kim murder-suicide, their stock underwriters predicted that the price rise on the first day would exceed expectations. Hyung's message to Tomoko before exiting was terse.

Go home, blossom. I will make sure you are not forgotten.

-What about Aeura?

He did not turn around. Tomoko locked the door and settled in. Something didn't feel right. Along with a pearl-handled pistol, she had packed a naughty nightie just in case. Tomoko was glad she had her gun. She unlocked its case, took it out, and loaded it.

Another knock on the door had Tomoko assuming it was Hyung, back to talk sense or sex. But it wasn't him. It was

Rodney Allan. The tanned and fit smooth operator, oozing his Beverly Hills charm, stepped in wearing tennis gear. With a wordless smile, he grabbed Tomoko's wrist and gently removed the pistol from her hand.

Up for a game?

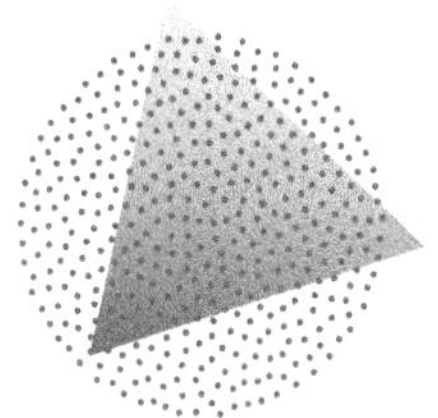

right now

We are scared, confined in the S&M chamber for far too long. In the thick-walled room, there is no phone or internet and no one can hear our cries. We ran out of smart-aleck jokes about the erotic furnishings long before VJ discovered the camera covered behind a spiked leather cowl on the wall. He had been planning to try it on and do a few Batman bits when he noticed a small hole in the concrete covered by the mask. It gives us hope and new conversation. Aeura flashes a middle finger to the camera.

They're watching us.

-Certainly it's on record. Good for the blackmail business.

Leticia knows her true crime angles. I know only frustration.

Rip it out!

-Hold on. It's connected to a Wi-Fi hot spot. I may be able to get a signal for us by piggybacking on it.

VJ has talent. I am always in awe. With concentration he gives it a whirl.

Got it. I'm on for the moment! I can email.

-Serious?

Leticia is impressed. So is Aeura. They are all about him. VJ takes the spotlight in stride. I feel a pang of jealousy. Damn. VJ seeks my advice, which helps.

Who gets the first Bat-Signal?

-Who do you think is still up? Duke.

3.

saturday night

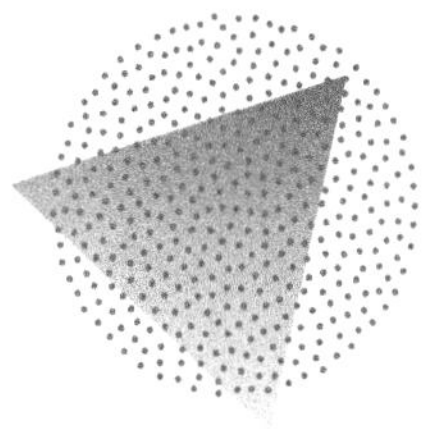

duke waf at fantafy ifland, the strip club near the 405 in West LA. He was ignoring all the enticing eye candy gyrating adjacent to him, concentrating instead on the inconvenience of this urgent-sounding email from Gilly's friend VJ. With a groan at the thought, he replied that he was finishing up something and would head out ASAP. He added they should contact Detective Boylan. Duke didn't plan to hurry for the Burbank Hills. He had been working on a crypto play of his own, which involved a rock-and-roll NFT, a non-fungible token.

He had invested in a digitized Jimi Hendrix film clip at a swap meet. Though he paid too much, Duke finally had a buyer at his asking price coming to meet him. It was weird that the offer didn't come through eBay but from his buddy who owned the Laurel Way house. The buyer was already half an hour late when he joined Duke at a table as arranged. He did not come alone. The two men were in suits and swarthy in complexion, dripping wet from a building rainstorm that was long in coming. An unhappy bundle of bad vibes, they got right to the point and handed Duke an address on a sticky note.

Pick up your son and his friends. They're safe for now, locked in a basement room.

That was accompanied by a warning for Gilly and company, harshing the mellow of the Duke. It was that unmistakable, in all caps. **LEAVE THINGS ALONE OR ELSE**. To emphasize the point, the bigger of the two men, whom Duke figured to be Eastern European, gave the pool man's shoulder a squeeze so hard that Duke felt it right down to his testicles, which rang in pain. He got the message and nodded his confirmation. The men left but not before Duke yelled out to them over the bump-and-grind music.

What about the Hendrix NFT?

Laughter was the only reply. Duke looked at the address on the note. It was the same as the one VJ had emailed him.

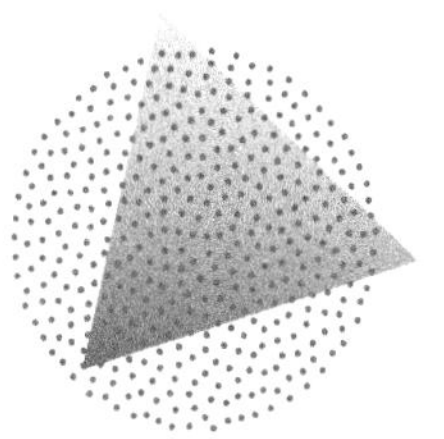

rigHt Now

 It's been a long day, and the body needs to recharge for what's to come. Whatever that is. Aeura's head is on my shoulder. Leticia's head is in my lap. VJ is trying to reconnect to the hot spot. He has not been successful since the first time. He is almost certain the one email went out before the signal bounced. I am trying to keep spirits up.

If they were going to harm us, they would have done it by now.

-What? So they just let us die of hunger and thirst?

Duke will be here. It's a ride but at this hour, thirty minutes maybe, and he will be unbolting that door.

--If they don't come for us before!

---Who are "THEY?"

We all have our suspicions and let them flow to kill the time. Leticia, used to being the debate club leader, takes each idea and tests its validity. We all agree it has to do with the IPO. Crypto Mining League. Even VJ likes the sound of that.

It's a winner. The financial mavens predict $11 billion for the owners.

Leticia prods. Aeura stands to get her bearings and then spills. Even rumpled and worn out she is beautiful. I catch VJ staring at her with the same eyes. Leticia sees me seeing VJ seeing Aeura. Why does love have to be so mad? Aeura takes a breath and tells all she knows about her father's dealings.

He and James Hyung were grad student roommates with a dream. After the original start-up, Dad went back to teaching data science in Hong Kong. He was a scholar, not a businessman or a killer.

Aeura reveals that in the early days her stepmother, Delores, provided the bridge funds that kept the company alive long enough to restructure and attract real attention and capital. The deal negotiated made Sidney and Delores equal partners in any sale with Hyung and Allan.

My father told my mother Hyung tried to force him out before the public offering was announced.

-That tears it for me.

Leticia is all in. The partners are greedy and do not think the Kims should get so big a share. It's textbook Occam's razor, she explains. The simplest explanation is the best. We are all on the same page. The troubling fact that the Beverly Hills Police Department does not see this motive as clearly as we do leads to the wrap-up.

They are in on it somehow.

-And the Armenian mob?

--Definitely have a lot at stake. For all the clumsy cover-ups, who is calling the shots?

My question seems to stump the investigative panel. Ear to the door, Aeura tenses.

Shh!

Someone is outside the portal. The bolt is rattling. I whisper caution.

It can't be Duke yet.

VJ and I frame ourselves around the door with whatever we can grab for weapons—a whip, a studded mask. The door pushes open with a flourish.

Ta-da!

It's Abby Jo and her friend Christina.

5.

Saturday Night

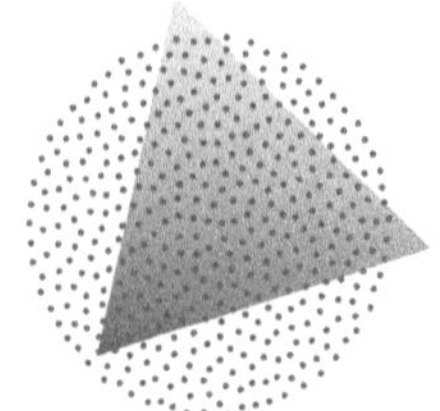

it had been a very hot and dry year for LA. Never a good combo. The first big fire of the fall, two months earlier, had denuded a lot of the Caheunga Pass. With no roots or brush to anchor the earth it was a recipe for calamity. The rain had been going for a few hours when Duke turned off for the Burbank Hills and then turned right around. Up ahead a cliff had collapsed and a mudslide had sealed the road in and out. Horns were honking to alert motorists. Emergency vehicles rumbled in as a local disaster zone was forming before his eyes.

Duke tried all the cell numbers he had for Gilly and VJ and got only voicemail. He knew a hairstylist who lived near and imagined he could seek refuge till it died down. He could have, but instead he went the extra mile— literally—for his boy. The whole business had gotten weirder, and he didn't want the kid involved another day. He parked the truck and made it up the hillside on foot, pushing through the hammering downpour toward the address.

Halfway up the hill, walking cross-country style with trees and shrubs as stabilizing poles alongside the rushing river of a road, Duke passed a black Tesla caught midway. It was headed downhill and had slid off the asphalt. It was wedged between a boulder and tree. Duke peeked into the car to see if he could be of help. The driver was slumped over the steering wheel, half his skull blown apart, leaking blood. Duke cleared the watery buildup on the driver's side window for a better view and noticed a pistol on the passenger seat. The dead man was a local hotshot he recognized from the news and from years doing Beverly Hills pools, hearing Beverly Hills gossip. His name was Rodney Allan. Duke could see firemen and police coming up to secure the ravaged area. He yelled down to them, waving his arms.

Someone needs help. Hurry!

Duke had done his civic responsibility and didn't wait around. He hoped this had nothing to do with Gilly and his friends, but he knew it did.

6.

right Now

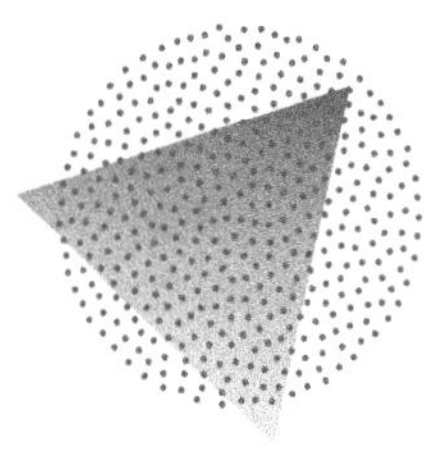

i AM ſo gLAd to ſee duke, ANd He iſ gLAd to ſee ALL of uſ uNHArMed. In this Burbank Hills bungalow, with the rain hammering on the roof, I introduce Duke around and feel some pride in having a cool dad who answers the call. Duke is predictably more attentive to our host than to Abby Jo, with whom he has a long history. Even if we were freed before Duke arrived, it doesn't matter. Duke is a champion and my friends appreciate it. Lightning flashes through the living room picture window. It illuminates our faces and they are beautiful. Thunder booms. A rare electrical storm is overhead. Aeura, Leticia, VJ, Abby Jo, Christina, me, and my dad together after midnight was not on anyone's bingo card. We all look so alive. Our cell phones are charging, and I want to burst out with thanks. So I do! Everyone echoes it. We are safe, protected by the road closure and the raging storm.

Hartunian headed down the hill before the real rain started. He won't be back tonight.

-I made it through.

Sayeth the Duke, who is still dripping wet, soaked through and through, warming by the gas fireplace.

Sweetie, his suit is worth more to him than taking my life. He can do that anytime.

Christina chills us back to reality. In a silk kimono with her hair up, she pours us tea. She is not much older than us and, truth be told, is the first prostitute I have ever met. Same with the others and we are all surprised how normal and vulnerable she seems, hosting us with refreshments at this late hour. We have all gone through a bunch, and a lot of it doesn't make sense. We have a ton of questions, and Aeura can't hold back.

Why was my mother's gun here?

-The gun? A friend left it for me. He said Hartunian's gone off the rails, crazy. I forgot it when Abby Jo and I fled. The beast came in right after you kids. He locked you in.

--And how did you and Abby Jo get away?

-My jungle vine.

VJ is all ears and quizzical brow. Christina gives away her getaway secret. Abby Jo embellishes, her palms still raw from using a rope swing out the back door that got them over to a neighbor's deck below.

I'm watering her plants while she's watching her grandkids in Grand Rapids.

-I can't believe I made it across. I think it was those three words Christina kept chanting: "Hartunian is coming!"

-You got it! Hartunian's a killer. He does mob wet work. With this deal he's aiming higher, going legit.

Abby Jo adds that tidbit, lighting up a cigarette. Duke bums one. Christina continues.

Hartunian was worried I knew too much. Rodney, my good friend, says I should go back to Serbia.

-If you mean Rodney Allan. He's dead.

Christina crumbles into the plush leather chair that engulfs her. It's a body blow. Duke, saint that he is, steadies her and gently takes her hand. He tells her what he saw near the bottom of the hill. A Tesla skidded off the slick incline, wedged in trees. The deceased Rodney Allan with a gunshot wound to the head. A gun nearby.

A suicide? Yeah, right.

Leticia scoffs too loudly and I explain.

There's a lot of sticky parts to this situation and not the first bogus suicide.

-Are you Sidney Kim's daughter?

Christina looks over to Aeura, and Aeura nods. Christina does know too much and rises to face the Korean American teen. She brushes away Aeura's bangs and plants a kiss on her forehead.

I'm sorry, dear. He didn't kill himself.

Aeura cries on hearing those words.

saturday Night, Later

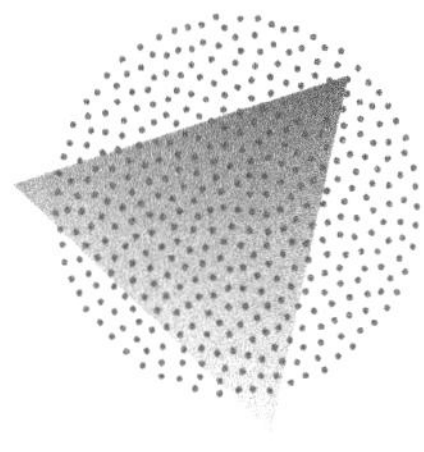

the exHAUſtioN LeveL WAſ off tHe cHArtſ. Everyone had crashed, hoping to get a few hours' sleep before the slap of daylight brought us to the harsh reality of our senses. With any luck the driving rain would never be over. Christina retreated to her bedroom, and VJ, the girls, and I took the other one. That left Duke and Abby Jo finding couch space in the living room. The second bedroom had one queen bed and a single twin. Leticia and Aeura collapsed onto the bigger one, which left me and VJ crowded out, sharing the other. Hugging the edges of the bed, back-to-back, VJ and I could hear Leticia and Aeura already off to dreamland, snoring faint as distant bells. I was falling into the last moment of consciousness, savoring the bliss, when I heard a guttural grunt from another room. It was a sound I had grown up with. VJ stirred and whispered.

What is that?

-Duke.

Duke?

The next sound ended the guessing. It was Abby Jo having one helluva orgasm. She hit all the notes, low to high, and a few that might have been lost for decades. She and Duke were bonking away. After that, it went all quiet. I knew better.

Wait for it.

VJ was wide awake. Leticia and Aeura were sitting up as well. Turned on, we waited like the sound voyeurs we were and were treated to Duke letting loose with his happiest orgasmic vocalization. It was impressive. Hilarity ensued. We couldn't stop ourselves rolling over in pain trying to stifle it. Listening with the others in the dark, I was amazed how unembarrassed I was. There was the quiet aftermath that followed. In the dark Leticia whispered to me from the other bed.

Is it over?

-Doubtful.

Duke did not disappoint. From beyond the walls Abby Jo went off again, sudden like a firecracker. Then a chuckle, some cooing, and silence. We all took a breath. I signaled.

Okay, it's safe. Good night.

As if sleep was possible. As if a future was guaranteed.

riGHt NOw

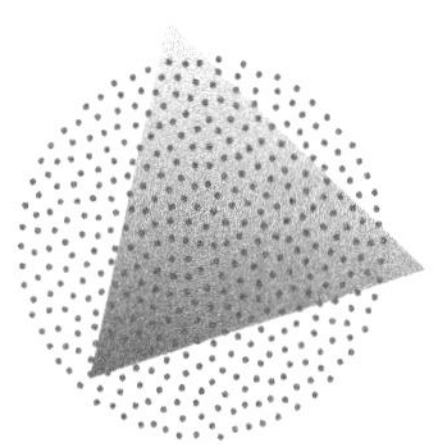

 I am bare-chested in the queen bed, sandwiched between Leticia and Aeura. VJ sleeps with one arm around Aeura. We are four abed, thick as thieves. I am the only one awake and can hear someone outside in the hall. I climb over Leticia and cross the floor in my underwear to peek out the door. Christina is dressed for travel, departing with a rolling suitcase. Out the front door she goes. Back in the room I slide the curtain aside and lift open the window. The rushing air is sweet like it always is after the rain. I smell pine and spruce from the hillside. Down on the street I catch a glimpse of Christina being helped into a dark Lexus. Not just any waiting car.

Detective Boylan!?

I repeat it loud enough to wake VJ.

Chill, dude.

-Christina just got into Boylan's car.

That gets Leticia back on the case and pumping with concern.

Abby Jo has to call her. It could be a trap! Gilly, go!

I spring out the door. Abby Jo and Duke are passed out on separate couches. I shake Abby Jo and she is not happy.

It's Christina. She got picked up by Detective Boylan. Is that cool?

-Shit! She said she was going to the airport. Unless he's also driving Uber, she's with him.

Duke hears this and vouches for Boylan. Then thinks about it and changes course. Abby Jo is half naked. I cannot unsee what I am seeing. Oh well. People should be happy, Duke always says, and Abby Jo sure sounded happy last night. Abby Jo unplugs her phone and tries to reach Christina. It goes to voicemail.

Hey friend, give me a call from the airport. Worried about you.

VJ comes in with news.

The Nextdoor app is blowing up: Dead man found in Tesla identified as Rodney Allan of Beverly Hills.

Word in the comments section is it's not being investigated as storm related. Duke feels obligated to take charge and urges us all to get dressed and off the hill. He passes on the warning from the gangster duo who came at him. He goes to Aeura, takes her hand, and is genuine and kind.

I think you should find your mother.

Dad is dead on. Sorry about that. Dad is spot on, and I don't have to rally my troops against the renewed danger. Everyone is up and dressed and secretly wondering what we did last night in that queen bed when the lights went off. I can say all I remember is the coziness of warm flesh on flesh and the intoxicating smell of two different types of shampoo.

Maybe the fragrance knocked me out, but I can state it was all pretty chaste. I will check with VJ later to make sure.

9

Sunday Morning

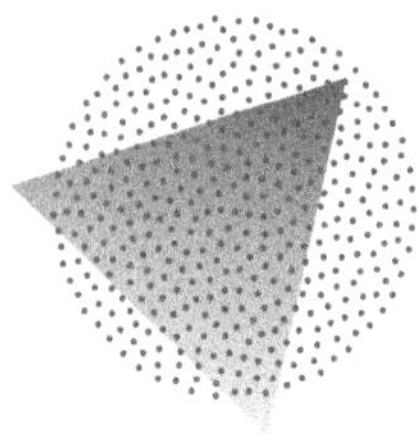

duke did the duke thing and suggested we all go Westside to Venice by the pier. Cool down, get some sea air, and thank that lucky old sun we are upright.

Breakfast at the Whaler on me.

Duke had a tab deal with the owner, whose Mar Vista pool he cleaned. Abby Jo was all about it and so were the others. We figured we'd do a pit stop at Leticia's place. Her mother wasn't due back till later on Sunday, and we all needed a refresh. Duke and Abby Jo went off ahead, and the plan was to meet them at the Whaler at the foot of Washington Boulevard and the sand.

Leticia and I strode ahead, out of the hillside cottage and down the walk to the street. Behind us, Aeura and VJ were caught up in an argument about what constituted Pacific Rim cuisine. The closer I got to Leticia's mom's SUV, the more my stomach refluxed. I could see the back passenger door was ajar. Eyeing it, Leticia gave my wrist a sudden squeeze. The car had been broken into. In the back seat was the blood-soaked body of our former host, Christina, propped upright with a seat belt restraint. Her throat had been cut. Leticia muted a scream. I was speechless. Aeura and VJ stopped, sensing our distress. Leticia's words squeaked out.

We have to call the police. He's a mad man.

I focused and scanned the area, knowing he could be watching our reaction. With an arm around Leticia's shoulder, I brought the others into a huddle to shield me while I punched in 9-1-1.

Yes, hello. Someone put a dead body in our parked car.

I gave the details, and we stayed close to the car, trying not to peek in at poor Christina. I knew Leticia thought she was killed by Hartunian. It seemed more his style than Detective Boylan. Except Christina had left for the airport with Boylan—in Boylan's car. If Boylan didn't kill her, where was he?

Down the hill, sirens could be heard getting louder. The message from the killer to us was unclear. Did he think we would not call the police after finding a body in our car? Did they not care?

Should I call my mother?

Aeura looked at me for approval. She had no *effs* to give.
Can't hurt. Everyone who is after us knows where we are.

* * *

Aeura's call to her dear mother came at an inopportune moment. Tomoko Kim, who'd traveled from Texas after learning of her ex-husband's suicide, was down on her knees trying her best to beg an old lover—the self-proclaimed mastermind behind the blockbuster crypto-mining IPO. James Hyung was losing patience with her. He needed her to sign away Aeura's claim. He'd given Tomoko a promissory note for a few million dollars and was not interested in negotiating anymore. The sight of the middle-aged woman throwing herself before him was a turn off. He was about to become a multibillionaire on Tuesday, with two fewer partners to share with, and he didn't need this baggage. The Armenian gang and its police network were enough of a sieve on his empire-building plans. He would have plenty of time for indulgences after the IPO was funded. With a swift jerk he pulled Tomoko up to her feet.

Answer your damn phone. And then sign and go home!

Tomoko took the call from Aeura and told her daughter to head to the airport.

What about Dad's friend, James Hyung? He either had Dad killed or is the next target!

-That's nice. See you soon.

Feeling Hyung's gaze, Tomoko tried not to draw suspicion and aborted the call. He handed her a pen and she signed the document. Handing it over, she shot James the sweetest, fakest look she could and left his office without a word. Crossing the pool area to the back gate, she was stopped by Detective Boylan, who had been lounging, drink in hand. He rose in her path and squared her up.

Your daughter's a liar and could be in big trouble.

-She's flying back to Houston.

That may not be far enough if she continues playing detective.

10.

riGHt Now

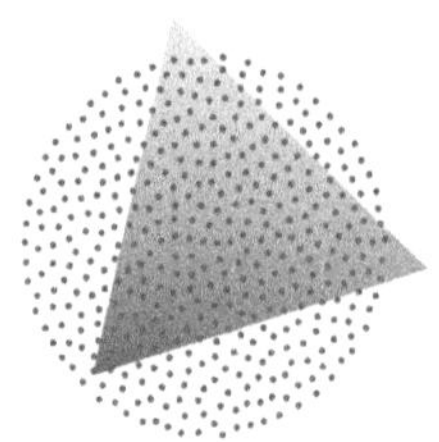

 It's already getting dark on this winter Sunday afternoon. The police questioned us separately for a few hours and were kind enough to bring in some lunch. None of us felt confident to talk of the conspiracy we know exists. Our story was consistent. Touring our friend from Houston around, we got stuck. We were orphans of the storm, riding it out for the night inside a friendly stranger's house.

We knew her name was Christina, nothing more. We had no

idea why she was placed in our car. Only we did. The message sunk in enough that we were tight-lipped till we could get some distance from danger and find someone to trust. The killers were counting on us dummying up, and we did not disappoint. The Burbank police made us all promise not to leave the county in the next forty-eight hours. That means Aeura cannot go back home to Houston with her mother. Leticia is on the phone trying to explain to her own mom that their car was impounded as evidence in a murder. Aeura cannot stay there with Leticia's mom bent out of shape. VJ's place is off-limits, too, with the strictest parents I know. I will ask Duke to let Aeura stay at our place. Should be cool. Especially if he is still with Abby Jo. She may have someone in the press for us to tell our story to. We can all share an Uber Black, so I punch one in. It is two minutes away.

VJ yawns and it's infectious. We are about to head to the Westside when Leticia goes rogue.

As soon as you leave, I am going back in to tell everything. My mother's going to kill me if I don't!

I cancel the Uber and explain to Leticia if she goes back in and tells all, we have to as well. And where do we begin the story? My doing the pool on Laurel Way? Aeura's father being falsely accused and murdered in the custody of the Beverly Hills Police Department? Or what about the kid from the bookstore? Another covered-up murder that no one is questioning. How do we explain the Glendale Armenian mob's role in this? How far-reaching is their ability to operate with impunity? They could have the Burbank cops within their grasp as well. Shit,

Glendale is Burbank's neighbor to the east. Do we dare tell them that on Tuesday these killers will make a killing and will stop at nothing to make sure they do? VJ and Aeura are silent, as uncertain as I am. They know if we go back in that police station we may never come out. Leticia tries to counter these points. VJ scores the debate with a clinching notion.

Guys, I'm going home to do homework. We have school tomorrow!

Leticia laughs and can't stop. Crazy what pressure we put on ourselves. Aeura whispers in my ear.

I am getting a hotel room. No matter what happens, stay with me.

I hit the rideshare app hard.

11.

ſunday, Late afterNOON

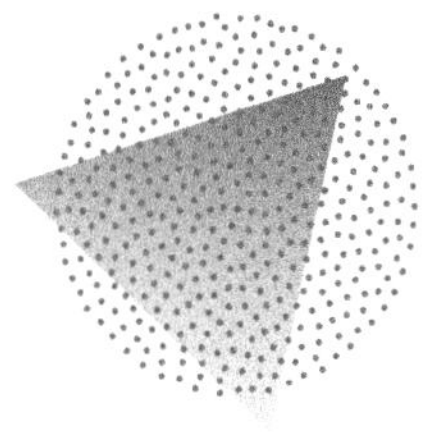

duke ſcored ſoMe HALibut froM a frieNd fiſHiNg oN tHe pier and was happily cleaning it back at the West LA digs. Abby Jo was at work on a medley of rice, mushrooms, and broccoli to bedrock the dinner. Duke thought we'd just flaked on him when we never showed for breakfast at the Whaler. We missed the famous Muscle Beach scramble and a local v. tourist fistfight over a parking spot in which Duke won a ten-buck bet and a pre-roll from his writer/surfing buddy Chuck. The day was bright. It changed the minute Aeura and I showed up to grab some clothes and her suitcase. They had no idea what had transpired.

Christina's dead?

-You found the body in your girlfriend's car?

--She's not my girlfriend.

Whatever! Those bastards!

Abby Jo was seething with the news of her friend Christina's sudden demise. Duke was looking for some solid ground, damage control on the situation.

What did you tell the cops?

-As little as possible. We don't know who to trust. Aeura can't leave the county, so she's got a room at the Peninsula Hotel tonight. I'm staying with her.

Duke glanced over to Aeura, mulling the situation.

Really? How old are you?

Aeura glared back, not asking for his permission. I pulled her in close. It's been an unreal few days. Duke backed off and returned to his fish. Abby Jo nodded approval, lit another cigarette, and noticed she still had one going in an ashtray. She stubbed them both out with a heavy dose of sarcasm.

The Peninsula. Sure, makes sense. Only a grand a night. Before tax.

I shrugged it off. Aeura's mother was paying, and we would be safe there. Duke was panning the fillet, trying to put together a way forward, when his work cell rang. It was his buddy calling in from Majorca. There was a problem with the Laurel Way house's pool heater.

Could be the temperature sensor. We're on it. Adios, amigo.

-Are you serious? You're going up to Laurel Way!?

I'm a pool guy, kid. That's what we do. Come on.

-Uh, no. Respectfully decline, sir.

--Duke, I'll help you.

Abby Jo had her reasons. I wasn't going to stop her, and I wasn't going to change my mind.

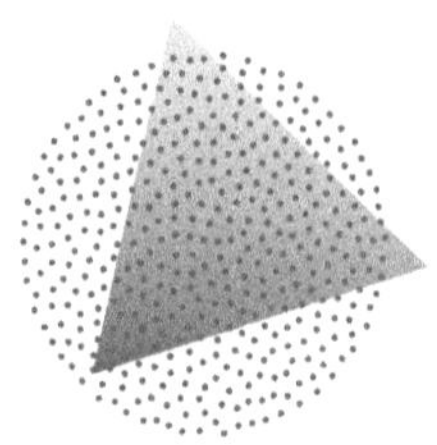

right Now

the peninsula hotel in beverly hills is swank, to use a term my mother loved to describe Rodeo Drive. The hotel's crystal-chandeliered lobby and modern design oozes class and opulence. Waiting for Aeura's mother, Tomoko, to meet us, I have uncomfortable thoughts. I should have gone with Duke. The guilt gnawing at me dissolves when Aeura smiles and tugs at my hand.

Here she is. Mom!

Aeura goes to her mother. Tomoko hugs back in a restrained way. I try not to judge through the lens of cultural bias—a woke concept Leticia had us bone up on for a debate. I hope Leticia is okay back at her house. I tried calling her but got only voicemail. Maybe my guilty pang is about her. Aeura introduces me, but Tomoko gives me little warmth or even acknowledgement. She gets us registered and I am thinking how odd this feels. She is putting me, a stranger, in a hotel room with her daughter, without any questions asked.

She and her mother walk and chat on the way to the elevator lobby, following a bellhop with Aeura's rolling suitcase and my backpack of essentials. I am thinking maybe her mom plans to occupy the room with us, which somehow makes some sense. However, she has come with no luggage, which kills that thought. We ride to the top floor, where the suites are located, each with two bedrooms, I am sure. The bellhop unlocks the door with a swipe and hands the key cards to Tomoko. She tips him with a twenty and tells him that he does not need to bring them inside. For the first time, Aeura's mother looks at me with purpose. Okay, making progress. I get the signal, take hold of the luggage, and stride in. The room is breathtaking, I can't lie. Aeura is impressed too. Her mother closes the door. I continue into the main bedroom and am greeted with a familiar face on a huge body sitting on the bed. Hartunian grins and my blood drains.

Make yourself at home.

Aeura enters, sees him, and backtracks, running for the exit door. Her mother blocks her, grabbing hold and shaking.

Don't be a fool. You must stay here. It's only till Tuesday. You too!

Tomoko makes two things clear to me. I will not be going to school tomorrow, and I should have really gone with Duke.

13.

SUNDAY NIGHT

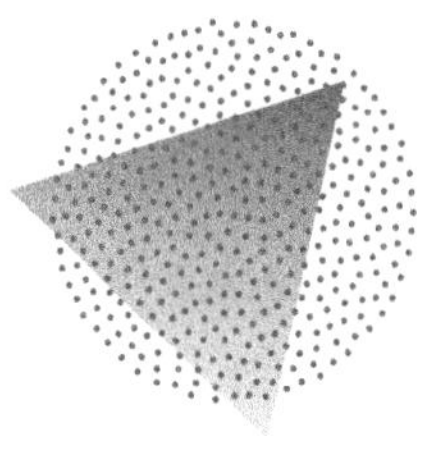

ABBY JO WAS SCREAMING TRUTHS as an intubated Duke was being hurried into an ambulance by two Los Angeles Fire Department EMTs. He'd been electrocuted changing a pool sensor and had to be resuscitated twice by Abby Jo, who had fortunately taken a free CPR class years before. Duke had survived a cardiac arrest. She was still shaking. The ambulance's rear doors closed, shutting her out as the vehicle started to hurry away, siren howling. The indie journalist/Gray Panther activist was faster. She blocked the ambulance by standing in the middle of the Laurel Way driveway, waving her arms until they had no choice but to let her ride along.

At Cedars-Sinai Medical Center on the edge of Beverly Hills, Abby Jo followed the rolling gurney into the Emergency Room. It was Duke's least-favorite hospital, the one in which my mother—his ex-wife—had breathed her last, as had others he knew and loved. Duke disappeared behind a curtain to be examined, and Abby Jo was left to her own demons. She knew Duke's electrocution was not an accident. She replayed every-thing that had gone down at Laurel Way.

They were waved through the back gate by a security guard Duke did not recognize. There were two young Korean girls lounging around the pool in cartoon-character bikinis. Their father, who introduced himself to Duke, was James Hyung himself. He was very angry that the pool could not be heated for his girls, considering what he was paying.

Duke went right over to the heater, saw the problem, and went to the pool to install a new sensor he'd packed. That moment was etched in Abby Jo's mind. Duke leaned over the pool edge. He reached under the water and was knocked back by a sudden electrical jolt, doing a near somersault and landing on the stone hardscape, his long gray hair crackling with fire. Abby Jo was on him to put it out, looking for help. She was met with the faces of the young girls. They were grinning—not surprised, not horrified. What was not lost in translation for Abby Jo was the fact Duke was meant to die. She had prevented it.

In the waiting room Abby Jo scrolled through her phone for the first call she'd made to Gilly that got her into this grisly business. She found the number and clicked. There was only voicemail and it was full. She remembered the kids were staying at the Peninsula Hotel and tried her best to get through to them there. The front desk was no help, no matter how many names Abby Jo dropped. She'd have to go down there in person. She caught one of the admitting doctors out in the hall, and he told her Duke had stabilized and was breathing on his own, resting. The ER doc was about Abby Jo's age and lacked the typical Beverly Hills airs. He praised Abby Jo's CPR rescue and encouraged her to leave.

We will know more in the morning. Get some rest yourself.

Abby Jo could swear he was flirting with her. Before heading out, she caught a glimpse of the waiting room TV on mute tuned to a popular business channel. There was James Hyung, with his $5K suit and perfectly coiffed black hair—his daughters on either side in matching polka-dotted outfits. He was talking to the camera, a crawl on the screen: *...Highly anticipated Crypto Mining League IPO to drop Tuesday despite recent tragedies...*

If the sound was on, she would have heard Hyung explaining that poor partner Rodney Allan had recently learned he was to be indicted on federal racketeering charges from a prior business and saw no way out. The pressure of an IPO launch is enormous. Hyung blames it for his old friend Sidney Kim's temporary insanity—murdering his wife Delores and then killing himself.

Hyung promised to dedicate the day to the two men who helped get the Crypto Mining League where it is today.

Abby Jo didn't need to hear it to know James Hyung was *evil AF*, as the kids say. And she was not afraid to *eff* him up in any way she could.

14.

right now

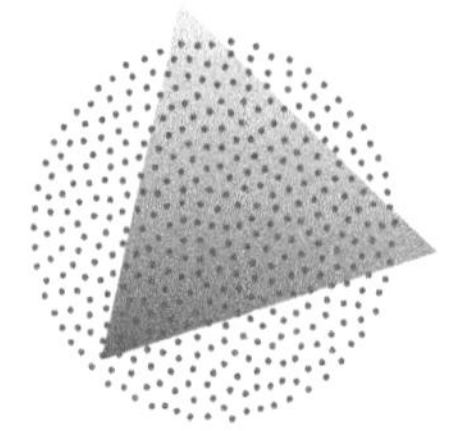

AEURA AND I ARE LOCKED IN THE SECOND BEDROOM with separate twin beds. It has to be after midnight. We have no phones—not our mobiles and not the bedside landline. They were confiscated, along with the unloaded pistol which Tomoko retrieved from Aeura's suitcase. I try to sleep and let time pass. I don't think they will hurt us here. Aeura is not herself. The betrayal by her mother, who appears to be part of the plot, is something Aeura cannot shake. I hear her weeping and it breaks my heart. There is nothing I can say at this point, but I try anyway.

We are going to be okay.

-No, we're not. We need an escape plan, Gilly. You can do it.

Oh shit. Okay, let me think.

The most obvious ideas rush forth. We fake a sudden sickness and when the guard comes, we overpower him and run for it. It's a trope always used in the movies, and the hero never seems to fail. Despite the cinematic success I don't feel it. A young, bearded guard who replaced Hartunian is armed, and the second room may have others still in it. We've heard voices. And then there's Tomoko. Is she still around? The windows don't open so there is no help there. The bathroom is a thought. A good thought. I spring out of bed in the dark and hit the bathroom light. There is a tub. I plug it and open the valve to let it fill up.

What are you doing?

-Flooding the bathroom.

The first smile in a long while cracks Aeura's beautiful, sad, pale face. She likes the idea.

If the water seeps to the floor below, it can alert housekeeping or management to investigate and shake up the status quo. We will have to be ready. The plan doesn't require scented bath crystals, but Aeura dumps in a ton anyway. The bubbles billow higher and higher for a nice Beverly Hills touch. It's stunning, actually, luxurious. The profligate waste. In no time the super suds are slopping over the marble edge. We take advantage of the moment to share a long, celebratory kiss. Halfway through its magic—my hands in places with Aeura they never were before—I get lost thinking of Leticia.

Aeura can tell there is a disconnect. She holds my head in her hands and looks in my eyes, my hands cupping her breasts.

What's wrong?

-What about Leticia?

What? You're feeling me up and thinking of Leticia?

-And VJ! Did they go after them too? Aren't they loose ends?

Aeura does not answer. She does not have to. She turns away with a shake of the head. I have harshed my own mellow and feel as clueless as a ten-year-old with bathwater up to my ankles.

At least something is going right.

15.

Monday, 2:17 a.m.

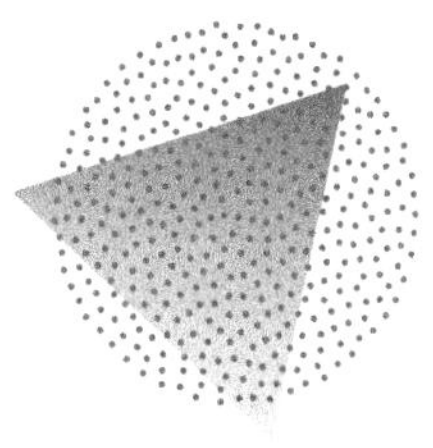

Alarms were erupting on the digital board behind the Peninsula Hotel's front desk. Blinking lights strobed red on the two uniformed night clerks saddled with an emergency on their usually tranquil graveyard shift. The young, fresh-faced strawberry blond whom Abby Jo had been pleading with, abruptly ignored her to call maintenance, sending them off ASAP, code red, to the top floor. The other clerk, a debonair Hispanic gentleman, who had snorted some coke on his break, was yelling for housekeeping to go to the third floor as he badly juggled calls from confused guests who had water coming through the ceilings of their rooms. Abby Jo could tell hell was breaking loose, and she hoped it had something to do with the kids. An auxiliary night squad of janitors who'd been cleaning the adjoining restaurant raced across the lobby, headed for the elevators with mops, buckets, and vacs in hand. Abby Jo followed.

On the fourth floor an assistant night manager with a gambling problem who had been checking the point spreads on the week's NBA games was summoned into action.

Meeting the call for fear of losing his job, he was knocking on suite doors to find the source of the water flow. He'd already awakened an irate Saudi media titan and caught a well-known game-show host half asleep with a woman half his age. He tried another door, knocking as politely as he could. The law of averages told him this would be it. He knocked again with more urgency than he intended. The young, bearded thug, shoes off, squished across the soaking carpet. He'd been sleeping too. He opened the door a crack and took in the skinny uniformed man who apologized, introduced himself—voice cracking—and explained the problem. He needed to come in and check. The assistant manager could feel the dampness and knew this room was the source of the water problem. The Eastern European henchman grunted an obscenity in a foreign tongue and told the hotel employee to get lost. The assistant manager surprised himself and grew some balls.

Let me in right now or I will call security!

Within the locked bedroom, Aeura and I could hear him. The bathwater was still rising. We readied at the silence, and then a husky, accented voice cut through.

Okay. Make it quick.

We took our places on either side of the door. The split second it opened we burst out. It stunned the assistant manager, who was nearly trampled and took a header into the gushing bathwater as we bolted for the hotel room's outer door. The guard was caught off guard and couldn't react quickly enough. In the hallway the elevator doors chimed, and out of the car rushed the janitor squad and Abby Jo in tight formation. Aeura and I ran for the exit stairs right past them with the young, bearded mobster in pursuit. God bless the old hippie—Abby Jo took one for the team, and with a swift arm move she lowered a janitor's mop handle and tripped herself, falling at the feet of our barefoot pursuer. The 250-pound hired muscle collapsed, taking a few janitors with him in a heap of buckets, mops, and vacs. Abby Jo wiggled away and shrugged.

Sorry. My bad.

In the stairwell I took the lead, two steps at a time down the four flights of stairs. We hit the first floor, changed gears, and sauntered with a wave toward the front desk as we exited the lobby into the darkness of the wee hours. I knew the way and Aeura followed, struggling to keep pace. We crossed Wilshire Boulevard sprinting and kept it up past the playground of El Rodeo, the snobbiest elementary school in the Beverly Hills public school system. Aeura couldn't run anymore and stopped me. Across the boulevard a flashlight's glow appeared and broke the stillness, followed by the sound of the incensed guard cursing at us as he crossed. Aeura quaked, spirit ebbing. I braced her.

Don't look back.

I took her hand, and we disappeared into an adjacent alley that lined the rear of the estates in the prestigious flats of Beverly Hills. Familiar ground for me. Duke and I worked a number of these properties. I stopped by a pair of imposing black-and-gold embossed iron service gates with an FF monogram. Reaching for the security keypad, I punched in a code from memory. Aeura tugged at my sleeve with frantic urgency. The keypad hummed and the gate unlocked. I slipped Aeura inside and stepped in, closing the portal behind me. The lock reset with a reassuring click.

The shoeless mobster, pistol out, huffed and puffed right by the black-and-gold gates. He looked around for a moment, confused, but kept going, feeling increasingly panicked about his own well-being if he lost us for good.

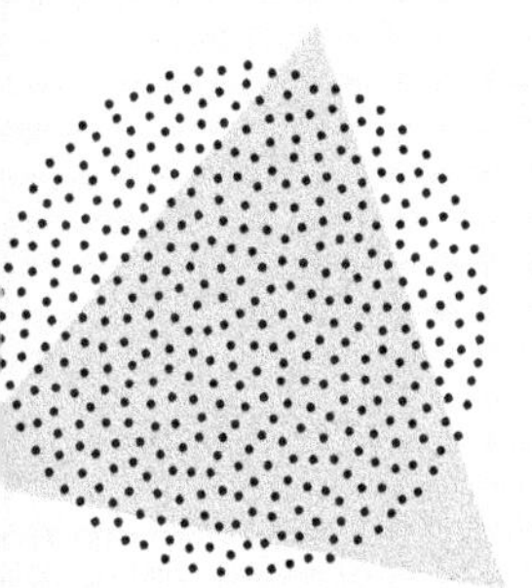

ferN

8.

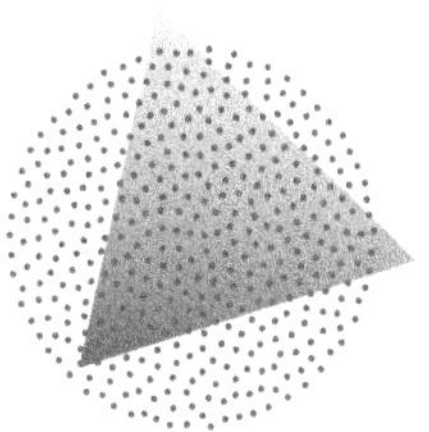

right Now

it's ALMOST dAWN, MONdAY MOrNING, aNd We Are covered iN pAtio furNiture tArps to stay warm in the chill of what's left of night. If I had my cell phone, I would be recording our latest predicament. Yet another place we are hiding out. How much longer can we keep this up? As poolside pump rooms go, the Fifer estate's is a palace. We have electric light, cases of imported bottled water, and even padded beach chairs. The Fifers are longtime clients of Duke's. They are third-generation Beverly Hills and represent the mega-moneyed Fifer Family Financial Fund. A phrase Duke loves to trill out for a laugh, repeating it faster and faster for effect. The only reason I remember the gate code is because it's so simple: 4-F-F-4. These people haven't had a worry for centuries. For a wealthy person, the head of the family, Phil, is always a pleasure to greet when we encounter him at the pool. His trophy wife is to be avoided, though Phil does insist she be kind to the little people like Duke and me. Fern, his only child from another marriage, takes after her mom in temperament and plastic surgery.

Thinking of Fern, I do get a little spark of happiness about the debate. It doesn't last. It leads to hard unknowns about VJ and Leticia. The day ahead should tell all. We will have to make a move soon. Nature calling and hunger and exhaustion are nagging at me. I should be getting ready for school, the last week before the Christmas Hanukkah Kwanzaa holiday break. One of the great school weeks where everyone's spirits seem to soar. I feel a hand brush my thigh and the body heat of Aeura is on me. She is stirring from a catnap, cuddles for a second, and then pulls away. Her hand traces around my face with distaste. My three-day stubble is like a speed bump under her delicate fingers.

It gets so scratchy. I hate that.

-Sorry. I didn't pack a razor.

I know. I...there's something I should tell you.

Oh boy. Can this be good? I feel I should buy some time and tell her it isn't necessary for me to know, whatever it is. Too late. There's no stopping her confession. Petrified at the preamble,

I brace for what's coming. Aeura explains that she attends an all-girls private school, always has.

Okay. Okay, and…

-All my serious relationships have been with girls. Without beards.

Oh. So you're a—

-Maybe. I don't know. I've never had sex with a boy.

Well then we're even. I haven't either.

Aeura laughs and it's music to my ears. I don't add the fact I've never had sex period. There could be time for that later. She is not done.

I mean, if we ever get free of this, I wouldn't be averse to trying… if you shaved. Wait. How can I even be thinking about this? We could be dead before lunch.

I like better the part about being free of this. There has to be someone to help us. Aeura leans over in her beach chair and kisses my lips with the most urgent intent I have ever felt. She pours herself into me as if time is running out. Is it? Carpe diem, I hear you.

Nothing has felt more right. I am tingling, squirming in my beach chair, and losing balance. Gravity does the rest. I topple backward into a shelving unit lined with pool toys. It teeters before crashing down. Silence returns but only for a second. A dog barks—and not a happy one.

Is someone there? Oh no!

A teenage girl's voice blends in with more ferocious barks coming our way.

Missy, stop! Stop! Who-ever you are, I am calling the police!

Busted, we open the pump house door and step outside

into the first rays of sun. It's Fern Fifer up early, walking her dog through the backyard garden, in silk designer pajamas and fluffy, rabbit-head slippers. She struggles to control Missy, an angry shih tzu bent on devouring us. I go retro and shoot a peace sign to her. The dog oddly calms.

Hi, Fern. I know you don't know me.

-You're Guillermo Montrose. The pool guy's kid. Ya. And you're the Jacuzzi Murderer's daughter.

--I haven't thought of myself that way, but ya.

-Fantastic. Come on inside. Meet my therapist.

We literally have to be asked twice.

Monday, 8:30 a.m.

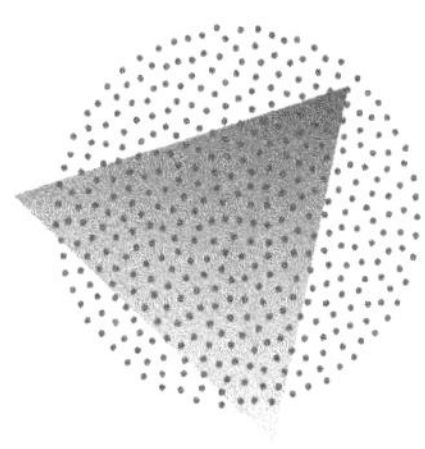

Downstairs from the grand lobby of the Beverly Hills Hotel is a vintage coffee shop. It is so low-key, it is no key. In the back corner, in a pink leather booth hidden from view, Carter Johannessen, the president of one of the most powerful PR firms in Beverly Hills, was yukking it up with James Hyung and Tomoko Kim. His firm was handling the IPO, and confidence in the launch was bubbling over. The conditional deals Carter has been party to in the last few days have ensured the opening day price will exceed even the rosiest expectations.

The idea thrills investors. Your ex-husband, like James, was a genius.

-*A troubled one. Wouldn't you say, Tomoko?*

--*Yes, a troubled one.*

Tomoko looked low, playing the part of a woman who'd been touched by tragedy. Carter patted her hand.

How is your daughter?

Carter could have been on a fact-finding mission or was making conversation as they were getting ready to leave. Either way, she lied.

All too much for her. On her way home.

Hyung nodded and they shared a look, thick as thieves. He had moved himself and his daughters to the hotel after the electrifying incident with the pool guy on Laurel Way. The PR maven reached for the check and shot a billionaire-boys'-club wink to Hyung.

Start working on philanthropic moves now. Get lovable.

Without looking up, Carter placed a credit card in the tray for the old, stone-faced server, along with five one-hundred-dollar bills. The dour waitress who'd seen it all warmed like a holiday bun and gushed gratitude, proving the point.

* * *

In Glendale the young, bearded henchman who let the two kids escape was being reamed out by the head of the Armenian mob. He was stripped of his trusted position and a whole nostril. His name was Arthur, and the fact that he was the *don's* namesake and godson did not pull any weight. A shiv, slicing through the flesh of his nose, was all he got. His scream was silenced by a dirty rag shoved into his mouth by a cousin. The message would reverberate through the ranks and the family.

Don't screw up!

Abby Jo has been at Cedars-Sinai Medical Center since the 7 a.m. shift change. She grinded personnel for news of Duke. So far, so good was the only response she got from doctors. It carried enough optimism to allow her to fall asleep in the waiting room. On the TV above her the local weather was playing, with the crawling banner: *...Santa Ana winds to hit Southland...* Video footage rolled on the TV, showing Beverly Hills city workers securing the fabulous Christmas decorations on Rodeo Drive. Abby Jo, stirred, found a cigarette in her bag and considered smoking right there. Instead, she got up and went into the women's bathroom to light up. Sitting on the toilet, she searched for a phone number, called, and coughed, dropping ashes between her legs into the toilet water.

* * *

Leticia was at home and in big trouble with her mother. So when her mother answered the landline call from Abby Jo asking for Leticia, she unloaded. She and Leticia had gone to the Burbank impound yard to get her car released, and Leticia was impounded instead. The teenager had been held at the Third Street Burbank Police station for over ten hours. Though it was bombastic, Abby Jo gleaned through a high-decibel rant that Leticia's mother had spent the entire ten hours herself in a dark hallway doing *Wordle* in between writing her ex to blame him for their daughter's behavior. Leticia finally had satisfied the detectives that she and her friends, unfortunate orphans of the storm, were not involved in the murder of Christina and she was let go. At that point Leticia wrestled the phone away from her mother, and Abby Jo learned that a cautious Leticia did not share with the police her suspicions of what was behind it all. Her mother yelled in frustration.

And what is behind it all, Leticia?

-Greed!

You watch too many murder shows!

✳ ✳ ✳

On time, VJ showed up for school. Going up the steps to enter Uni High that Monday morning VJ thought he saw an older, hulking figure outside the school gate watching him. He prayed like the *Game of Thrones* nerd he was to the "Old Gods and the New" that he was just imagining things.

right Now

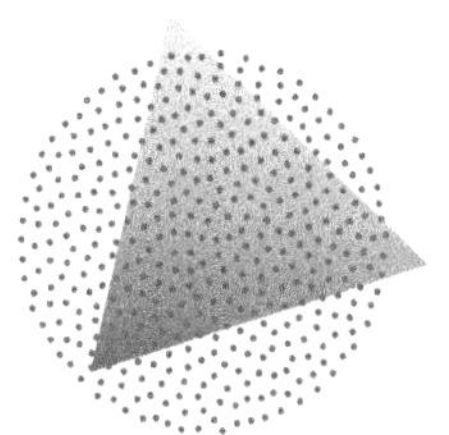

 in a kitchen bigger than my and Duke's whole apartment. Margarita, the Fifer cook, is making us waffles. Real waffles from scratch. Sitting at the gold-trimmed marble counter bar, we've had cappuccinos and biscotti, and the smell of bacon is in the air. A two-course breakfast. Who knew Fern's mother was a sworn enemy of Rodney Allan? The *late* Rodney Allan. The enemy of your enemy being your friend, Fern is not shy about filling us in on the reasons.

He roofied my mother when she was in college.

Fern's therapist, Dr. Guttenberg, has to be eighty years old and has been listening to the Fifer family secrets for half a century.

-Rodney was in my care at one point so I must honor that. I can say that if he was involved in this business, it can't be kosher. He cheated his own mother in a tax scam, and he loved her.

Balding, with trimmed facial hair, Dr. Guttenberg looks separated at birth from Sigmund Freud. A hungry Freud, the good doctor is first in line for the waffles. And I thought we were hungry. I wonder if he lives here, giving twenty-four-hour advice in a post–COVID-19 solution. Aeura wonders how her father could have gotten involved with Rodney Allan. Could he have been that naïve? This is torture for her and I consider holding her tightly, but Fern beats me to it. The Beverly Hills Barbie is really surprising me. Aeura appreciates the warmth in her gesture.

My father was a brilliant mathematician. James Hyung made the deal with Mr. Allan.

Aeura spits that out with disdain. She pats Fern's hand. Why do I feel jealous? Fern reveals that like Leticia and VJ, she has been burning up the internet to find what she can about the case. It's an obsession for her, she says. For us, it is an unsettling reality. More analog than digital. Scary. Fern focuses back on me and ups the wattage with a conspiratorial smile and a whisper.

My father doesn't trust the Beverly Hills police. They cover things up.

How could I have been so wrong about Fern? She gets it like I do. I dab my mouth and meet her smile with my best. I can feel Aeura's startled glance. Is she jealous?

Why were you hiding in my backyard?

In between more forkfuls of heavenly, light-crusted batter bits soaked with 100 percent Canadian maple syrup, I wrap up the CliffsNotes version of our greatest hits.

We were kidnapped and held at the Peninsula Hotel. Got away and ran.

-Before your father was electrocuted at that pool on Laurel Way?

I am paralyzed. Not sure that I heard right. I replay her words in my head in slo-mo and sit down. Fern feels terrible. She thought we knew.

He's not dead!

4.

MONDAY AFTERNOON

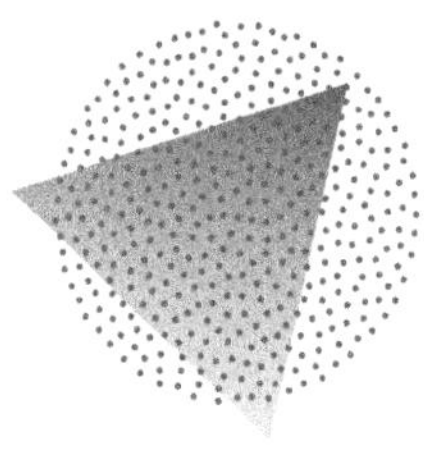

ABBY JO HELD UP THE HOSPITAL'S BEDSIDE PHONE TO DUKE'S EAR SO HE COULD HEAR ME. The pool guy's hair had been cut to eliminate the burned patches, and a surgical skullcap now graced his dome. Elevated on pulleys, his hands glistened with healing salves. The shock had knocked him unconscious, stopped his heart. Though light-headed on beta-blockers, Duke relayed to me that he was speeding toward life's exit ramp but had hit the brakes and made a U-turn.

I couldn't leave you an orphan, Gilly.

Crying and talking on the phone, Duke couldn't stop the gush. He went on in detail about the visions he had and transitioned to the exquisite beauty of Cedars-Sinai's huevos rancheros without missing a beat. Abby Jo took back the phone to talk to me herself.

Are you safe?

--*Yes. Thanks, Abby Jo! You helped.*

In the flats of Beverly Hills, I was alone in Fern's father's home office using the landline phone. Abby Jo coughed and laughed.

Believe me, every black-and-blue mark on my tuchis swears to it.

-What do you think we should do?

For your sake and your dad's, do nothing.

Abby Jo told me she was watching the hospital TV and caught the business-news channel's report on the week's IPOs.

They did a feature on the bad luck plaguing Aeura's father company. The publicity only drove the opening price higher. Pigs!

Aeura peeked her head in, and I gave her a nod of assurance. Abby Jo was asked to step out while a pretty nurse prepared to wash Duke down, pulling the covers back.

Oooo! You father is naked with a...

-With a what?

Let's just say his favorite organ woke up. Way up.

That's my dad. I felt a whole lot better, which was weird. Before hanging up, Abby Jo reiterated for us to lay low.

Let them make their billions Tuesday. The truth never ages.

* * *

-I like that.

I calmed down after the call. I would have asked the Fifers permission to take a shower, but Fern blocked the office door and whispered, accentuating each syllable.

The police are here!

5.

right NOW

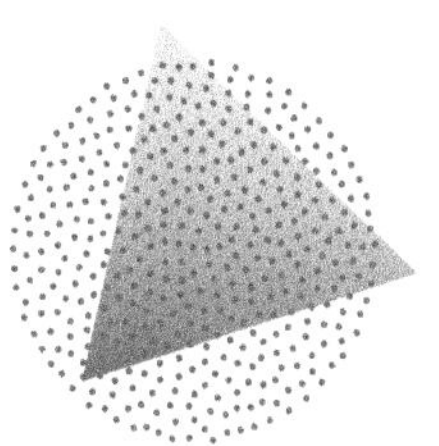

 Dr. Guttenberg is talking to them. Fern and I are huddled tight watching the scene in black and white on a small security camera monitor in a closet alcove in her father's office. We can't hear what they are saying and wonder if they could be looking for Aeura and me. Dr. Guttenberg is laughing and the cops follow suit. That is promising. I am physically closer to Fern than I ever have been. She has a wonderful scent of oranges about her, with a hint of jasmine. I am a Southern California boy. Orange blossom and blooming jasmine are in my DNA. I get a little too close, savoring the sensation.

Sorry. I love that smell.

Fern backs away with a wicked smile.

Are you flirting with me?

-What!?

You are. Player!

She says that with mocking admiration—but admiration nonetheless. She lets me off easy. She has not forgotten I destroyed her at the debate meet.

I deserved that for mailing it in.

On the black-and-white security monitor a super-hot lady in the latest exercise gear is seen coming up the stately path to the front door.

That's Natalie, my stepmother.

Natalie, fresh from a workout, sparkling with sparkle, joins the conversation with Fern's therapist and the police. Inside, Aeura creeps into the office and whispers with intensity to Fern and me.

They're looking for two teenagers who vandalized the Peninsula Hotel!

-Anyone we know?

I try to keep it light, feeling protected within the mighty walls of Fifer. From a hallway, stepmother Natalie yells to stepdaughter Fern and the walls come tumbling down.

Fern, why are you skipping school?! Did damn Dr. Guttenberg give you permission again?

We hustle out of the alcove to scatter, but it is too late. Natalie, who is either a trophy wife or a MILF or both, sees us. Her jaw drops with recognition.

I am telling the police!

-Natalie, no!

6.

MONDAY, 11:55 a.m.

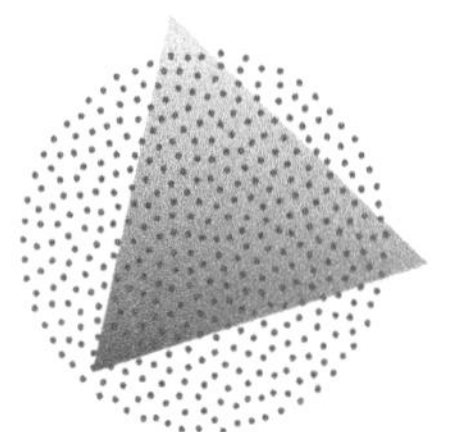

 a police sergeant handsome enough to be a TV star took us through the photo and fingerprint routine. It was my first time and Aeura's too. We shared a lot of reassuring looks, and the odd thing was we were not at all frightened. It felt easier than being on the run. We were charged with felony vandalism and told that because of a case backup we would not have a bail hearing till the following morning. Conveniently for the killers, that charade would happen after the IPO launch, which was set to go off at the Wall Street bell—6:30 a.m. Pacific Time on Tuesday, according to Aeura. Our hearing would be hours after Hyung made his megabuck haul and possible escape. I figured he had to be the one behind it all. But were there others pulling his strings? Aeura didn't say much about her mother anymore. It was obvious the divorcée from Houston had swung with Hyung over Aeura's well-being. That had to be deadening if you let it get to you.

Aeura and I were taken to different hallways after I had used up my one phone call on a hospital switchboard snafu. Aeura never got through to her mother. I was served lunch, a macaroni and cheese dish, and was expecting a visit from a court-appointed attorney. Being a juvenile in Beverly Hills, I was in a not-terrible-at-all holding cell with only one other guy. He was DeShawn, a Black kid, a skateboarding tagger who took a dare too far. We both agreed the mac and cheese was the bomb. I hoped Aeura was as comfortable. And the best part: I felt safe. Something I had not felt since I cleaned that pool on Laurel Way.

Aeura's holding area was even nicer than mine. Her cellmate was a fabulous, young, cross-dressing shoplifter who insisted on being treated as a girl and got her wish. Aeura and she/her were happy to talk punk fashion.

And the minutes went by. I say *minutes* because before my lunch tray was removed, I said goodbye to DeShawn, wished him luck, and was escorted out of the cell the same way I had come in. At the intake window I was handed back my belongings and shared a confused AF look with Aeura who was getting her stuff too. I was best-case scenarioing it and going with the idea that Fern's father arranged for this. He had old-money power in Beverly Hills, and Duke had asked him once to fix a speeding ticket and he did. A young, fresh-faced, college-aged guy in a suit escorted us out. He introduced himself as Brad and before we could ask a question, he answered.

The Peninsula Hotel apologizes. The charges against you were dropped. Come, Mr. Fifer wants to meet you.

-No shit?!

I said out loud what I was thinking and felt it came out wrong. I apologized.

You can't take the West LA out of the boy.

Aeura laughed and we waved goodbye to our jailers, exiting into the dumb sunlit air of the jewel of the Westside. It was joyous. There was a stretch limo waiting, and Aeura and I were ushered into the plush interior. Brad sat up front next to the uniformed driver, and before he closed the partition window he asked for our lunch orders. Mr. Fifer was getting takeout from Mr. Chow on Camden, and we were handed menus. I knew it by heart since my mother used to work there. Even though we had already feasted on mac and cheese I was not about to pass this up. I ordered for Aeura and me: Mr. Chow's insane salt-and-pepper prawns and the even sicker water dumplings, my mother's favorite.

And two Fiji waters.

Aeura added, handing back our menus. The window hummed shut and we were alone. Aeura couldn't help herself. She started tickling me and it was war. Giggling, carefree, living large, we were. The limo cruised Little Santa Monica Boulevard under the over-the-top cheesy but classy holiday lights that spanned the roadway. Christmas carols were chirping from a storefront. I once read in a novel about Hollywood hopefuls that when you move to Beverly Hills it's important to understand the difference between Santa Monica Boulevard and Little Santa Monica Boulevard. When I repeated it to Duke, he thought it was hilariously true.

It's the nuances there. Little is not little, value wise.

I couldn't wait to call Duke again. Someone had tried to kill him. Or kill me. The air conditioning was on, but the leather seats were chilly no more. Aeura had squeezed next to me for warmth, and I felt the festive, seasonal spirit permeate my body at last. I was thinking it was a day we earned, when Aeura had to harsh it and whisper.

What does Mr. Fifer want?

My every answer to that question seemed inadequate, frivolous, or illogical under the lethal nature of the circumstances. I tried an out-of-the-box stab.

Maybe Fifer is the guy behind it?

-Fern's dad? You're kidding?

Of course I am. Of course.

I wasn't just kidding—I was joking, feeling free and easy. Thinking about salt-and-pepper prawns. Aeura's body next to mine, the smell of Fern, and Leticia's kiss. School, where I should be, goofing between classes with VJ. Anything and everything but why Mr. Fifer wanted to see us.

7.

right Now

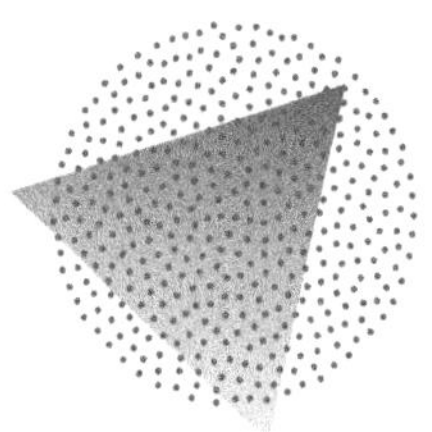

We laugh at Mr. Philip Fifer's witticism. We are in the executive lounge at Van Nuys Airport. It's an exclusive area for those with private planes like Mr. Fifer. He is dressed like he just got off the golf course at Hillcrest (which he did) and is flying to New York City as soon as his jet is ready. We thank him for getting the Peninsula Hotel charges dropped and for freeing and feeding us. Brad, Fifer's guy, stands at attention and watches us eat. I can't help myself and speed up the bites, feeling pressure. Fifer motions us to slow down.

Don't mind Brad. He worries we keep to schedule. How's your lunch?

-Couldn't be better.

--Yes, we really appreciate your kindness. Mr. Fifer.

Aeura looks at him sincerely. He takes her hand and gives it a reassuring tug, a gracious host. He is younger than Duke but has less hair, a fact the old man would definitely stress. I have never been in a lounge at any airport and feel a little intimidated. Not Aeura, as she has grown up in wealth and is as relaxed as I have seen her. Fifer finally lets go of her hand.

You have your mother's good looks. Hopefully your mother's good sense.

This sticks in my throat and makes the water dumpling hard to swallow. I know Aeura is caught off guard too. Mr. Fifer swigs down some red wine and motions to me with great magnanimity.

Ever been to New York for an IPO launch?

-No. I mean…of course not.

Wish I could take you along too.

-That's cool, Mr. Fifer. I have school tomorrow, and for real, these angry gangsters are kind of after us, sir. Did Fern not tell you?

She did. I'm sorry to hear that.

The lounge door opens, and James Hyung and Tomoko Kim are shown in by a pretty, uniformed flight attendant.

Ah, our other passengers have arrived.

Aeura grabs my arm and squeezes so tightly blood flow stops. Brad the efficiency robot opens the double doors to the jetway for the flight attendant who yawns, disappearing beyond.

Fifer rises.

Let's get this show on the road.

-Come, sweetie.

Following Fifer and Hyung, Tomoko reaches for her daughter with a maternal smile that is not fooling anyone. Aeura digs her boots in and does not budge.

What about Gilly, Mom?

-He's staying behind with Brad.

Mr. Fifer answers that with a nod to Brad as he exits through the jetway doors. He's followed by an impatient James Hyung. The smooth operator barks back at Tomoko.

Grab her!

I don't know how to read who is in more danger, Aeura or me. I take a step backward, toward the lounge entrance. I beckon to her, mouthing her name.

Aeura...

-Aeura! Continue along with your mother. Now!

Brad is louder, with an ugly black .45 Automatic pointed right at me. That drops the temperature in the room. Everything unfolds in slow motion. Aeura looks in my uncertain eyes and complies. Tomoko hurries her daughter toward the jetway. Brad lowers the gun into its holster.

Smart.

-No! Aeura, stop!

Those words aren't coming from me, and I am not hallucinating. At the lounge door is Fern Fifer in Fendi maroon leather pants and jacket, with a polished pink revolver in her hand trained on Brad.

Don't move!

Brad laughs, his eyes on Fern, his hand inching toward his chest holster.

Is that a toy?

-It's a Charter Arms Chic Lady, .38 Special. Hannukah present from dad, with private lessons. Go ask him what kind of shot I am. Hands on head, putz!

She trains the gun on his groin. Brad obeys. Aeura breaks free of her surprised mother and rushes to me. We gather behind Fern like a shield and all run frantically for the door.

Out front Fern rushes us to her Mercedes hybrid parked in a red zone. Before I get in the back seat, I can't help but ask.

Putz?

-Brad is.

What are you doing, Fern?

-Helping my father. Get in.

monday, 3:05 p.m.

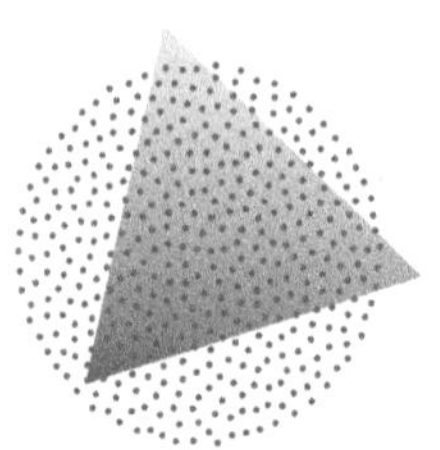

university high's old bell rang with purpose, and the school day ended. Leticia caught up with VJ. In case they were being watched he was not going to leave the main building until a critical mass of students exited. It did not take long.

Students poured into the lobby, heading for the door. Leticia and VJ lost themselves in the throng heading for the parking lot. VJ had gotten my text from Fern's cell and replied with a yellow-toned thumbs up, a confused face emoji, and a ha-ha one. Leticia was relieved Aeura and I were okay, and they both wanted to catch up. I texted back the address in Malibu where Fern was hiding us. It was right off the Pacific Coast Highway, north of Broad Beach, near the Ventura County line.

Is there anything we can bring?

-Well, since you asked, bro.

* * *

Duke was being processed for release from the hospital, and Abby Jo was running interference with the hospital staff to facilitate. She also was being cautious. The whole bloody business was about the stupid crypto IPO, and its debut was looming—less than a day away. She agreed with Gilly that it would be best for them all to be together while they were still at risk. She wheeled Duke out to the Cedars-Sinai pickup area and waited for VJ to come by to get them. A paparazzo outside hoping for a post-op sighting of a housewife of *The Real House-wives* took a shot of Duke instead. While lighting up a stub, Abby Jo went from zero to bitch in a millisecond.

Hey, parasite! What do you think you're doing?

-That's the pool guy who was electrocuted, isn't it?

--Tamp it down, AJ. Chill. Guy's trying to make an honest buck.

Duke posed for the shooter, loving the attention. He pulled a protesting Abby Jo down onto his lap, and she covered her face with her coat.

Not good, Duke.

-Hey, if they were after us, there would be some big hairy dude lurking.

Abby Jo peeked out from beneath her surplus army jacket and scanned the loading zone and beyond. She didn't see anyone. With a bright honk, VJ rolled up in his immaculate first-gen Prius. They loaded Duke into the car and were off for Malibu.

From the shadows a big hairy dude emerged and took serious note of the shiny old Toyota heading down the exit ramp to the street.

* * *

After we were rescued from the lounge at the Van Nuys Airport, Fern took us through the most beautiful of the Malibu canyons—Kanan Dume Road—to one of her mother's properties off the Pacific Coast Highway. It was a trip. A Pierre Koenig–designed beach house that the missus got in one of her three divorces. We were sitting by the pool, which was by the ocean, and I was doing my best to clean the sucker, which had clearly not been maintained in months.

She's been depressed and neglecting things, like paying bills. She still loves my dad and is worried about him. He made a mistake.

Even though we were the only ones around the pool on this remote stretch of private beachfront, Fern whispered. The Fifer Fund was underwriting the Crypto Mining League IPO through a shell entity, an L.L.C. Her dad didn't trust the auspices of the IPO to put it through the front door of his own company. Instead, he sometimes used the off-brand business to pump and dump a stock he didn't want to be connected with. But he changed his strategy. He grew to love the unique crypto idea and last month came out in public with the other partners to help with the launch through his legacy fund.

Did he know my father?

-In his desk drawer I found a photo of them together at a crypto conference last year.

Fern took it out of her $2K Gucci purse and handed it to Aeura.

He thought your father was so bright.

-He was. Thank you.

--You did your homework, Fern.

My mom's divorce turned me into a forensic accountant and all-around snoop.

--You are nothing like I thought. So glad to meet you.

Me too.

-Me three.

Aeura chimed in.

Fern brought out some pinot noir with a Napa Valley story attached, but I abstained. Not a drinker—though an occasional midnight toker—I got enough strikes against me just being born on the wrong side of the freeway to indulge. Aeura and Fern filled their crystal glasses and clinked, toasting each other as wine sisters. I didn't want to read anything into that. The sun was going to set right down in front of us. A special performance of fire meets sea. I felt like a millionaire, which isn't much in this town, but the sunset still resonated with Duke and me. It got granular after that, with Fern pouring her heart out and filling in the holes of the whole scary business. Her dad got suckered in before Rodney Allan was added. Her mother warned him and so did others at Hillcrest, but it was too late. He had to protect his investment.

Dad was not himself after he heard how your stepmom was poisoned in the Jacuzzi.

That last part Fern directed my way. Aeura defended me.

Gilly had nothing to do with it. He was with me.

We were each other's alibis. Bound together forever with the truth. Fern poured another glass for Aeura and for herself. There was some giggling. I tried not to judge. Besides, I was getting worried about where the others were. Fern wasn't done explaining her actions.

Your father's suicide had my dad unhinged. Dr. Guttenberg told me it was guilt, making him seem desperate. That's when I tried to find out more.

-*My father didn't kill himself or Delores Sung.*

You know that for a fact? Is that why they want you out of the way?

--*Can we get internet here? It's all on TikTok.*

I had the goods, but Fern's mother had her internet and modem turned off. Wandering down to the water's edge with Fern's cell, I got 5G on the shoreline, logged in, and searched TikTok for the K-pop twins' videos. I yelled to the girls.

No clip there! It was deleted!

Fern and Aeura groaned.

But I saved a copy in my Favorites folder!

Fern and Aeura cheered. I felt a burst of appreciation. Behind me, not too far out, twin dolphins breached the ocean's edge and perfectly arced, lit up by the colors of dusk more awesome than any double rainbow.

I rejoined the girls to show Fern the clip with the telltale chlorine jug in evidence. I plopped down between Aeura and Fern on a three-person wicker love seat with fluffy, floral print pillows. Ah! I could hear Duke's decent falsetto ringing in my brain with that classic, "Surf City" refrain, "Two girls for every boy."

My father's guy, Brad, is taking his orders from the Hyung guy, not from my dad. I overheard him on the phone.

-Did you tell your father?

Of course. He said he knew and to stay out of it.

--Glad you didn't listen.

He's not a criminal. You two can help clear him. You have to!

right Now

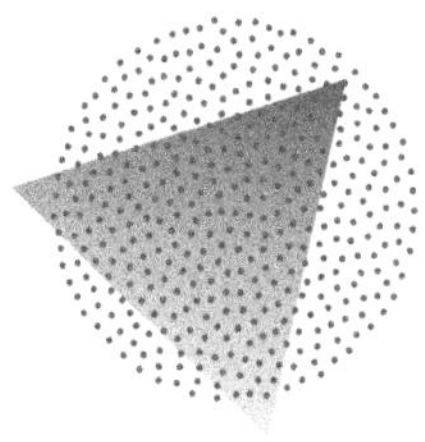

duke is hugging me, his hands in surgical gloves held out, pointed up like a prayer. With a skullcap on he looks like a religious leader and plays the part for my amusement. It's a moonless night sky. Under the hand-carved driftwood doorway to Margot Ross Fifer Day's beach house, he kisses my cheek. I wave them in. Duke is upbeat, smells the sea air, and lets out a mighty sigh.

Ah, crazy shit, Gil. Listen to Abby Jo. She knows.

-I think the kids are closer to it than we are, Duke. Time to listen.

We usher Duke and Abby Jo in, and the hugs continue with Leticia and VJ following. Looking over my shoulder, Leticia whispers in my ear.

Is that Fern Fifer behind that nose job?

-Behave. She is a warrior. VJ, what took you so long?

--You can thank me and your dad. We got takeout from Gladstones on his card!

-Pro move, Pop!

VJ's arms are full of steaming bags. Duke takes a bow and gives a surfer salute. Fern welcomes them and the intros are sweet. It would be so nice if this were happening under different circumstances. We dig into the Gladstones giant Fisherman Platter of fried goodies from the sea and a bucket of the signature lobster mac and cheese.

Gilly the Kid's favorite.

-It rocks. Thank you!

Aeura says that with a mouth full of macaroni. She is tipsy. Leticia asks to try the fries and Aeura hand-feeds her one. Leticia holds out a glass.

I think I have some catching up to do. Wine!

-Adult in the room. You're underage.

-It's all we have here. You can't drink the water.

More glasses come up. VJ and I drink wine. The tasty meal is one of the all-time *sickest*, and before we can even burp, Leticia nails us down.

Six-thirty a.m. our time their IPO will go live.

-Party! There's a champagne breakfast watch at my dad's office on Wilshire and Rodeo. It's always a sensational time for all involved.

Wonderful. How can we ruin it?

Fern takes offense at this, but I like Leticia's righteous indignation. She catches me admiring her and I don't look away. It does not go unnoticed by Aeura and Fern. Abby Jo echoes Leticia's notion, stubbing out a cig.

What she said! Ruin 'em, yes! Expose the swine!

-Not my dad. He's innocent.

--So was mine!

Duke raises a surgical gloved hand. He has a question.

They tried to kill me. Chased you. Why have they stopped?

-Can't we enjoy the fact they've forgotten us?

--Have they, VJ? I think we need to stay on guard.

---What he said.

Aeura has my back. I believe what I say. There is too much at stake for us to be a loose end.

I'm with Gilly too. We are the poop in the pool. Offense is the best defense.

-Thank you, Duke.

I feel supergood that my friends get to experience more Duke. He might not be the most successful guy, but he is the coolest. Like he says, he's been to the party a long time.

Fern's phone rings with a classical melody. It's an urgent call from Dr. Guttenberg. We do not hear what he is saying, but it is no news at first and then better news. Fern is nodding and giving us a thumbs up. She clicks off and fills us in. Her father is in New York and wants Fern to know. He's arranged for Detective Boylan to keep us safe.

We need to let him know where we are. I have the number.

-*No! Why didn't your dad call you direct, Fern? It's a trap!*

What!? No way!?

--Every which way!

Abby Jo outshouts everyone.

Boylan. Is. Dirty!

With a serious exclamation mark, all the power in the house goes dead. We are in darkness. No one even breathes. Aeura grabs my right hand. Fern my left. I can feel Leticia up against my back, lips in my ear, unafraid, whispering.

No matter what happens, I love you, Gilly.

Just as abruptly the lights bang on. A hearty howl of joy fills the dining room. VJ jokes.

Maybe your mother didn't pay her electric bill.

-*My mom is the worst at paying bills, so I put all her utilities on autopay.*

The lights flicker once, twice, and go out again.

Think positive.

This from Aeura, of all people.

Huddled in the dark, we think positive till we don't. Abby Jo's lighter sparks. Our faces are exposed. There is panic within me.

Did we lock the doors?

MONDAY, 11:03 P.M. EASTERN TIME

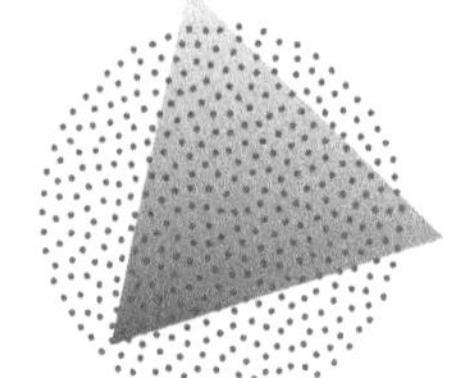

ON THE EAST COAST THE ELEVEN O' CLOCK NEWS HAD MOVED FROM AN ATTACK that took place on the subway to a fire in the Bronx. In the bedroom of a suite at The Plaza, Phil Fifer shut off the TV and hit the head before turning in. He was not alone. He was being babysat by an Asian security guard put in place by James Hyung. Relaxing on a couch in the adjoining sitting room, the wiry guard concentrated on a Kindle. At the sound of Fifer's cell going off on a side table, he grabbed the phone and carried it into the bedroom and then right into the bathroom. He joined Fern's dad who was on the toilet and handed him the chiming phone.

Answer it.

A billionaire who was used to giving orders, Fifer did as he was told. He certainly felt the pressure of the tightly wound Asian who looked like an MMA bruiser. He knew his loved ones could be in danger if he did not obey. He took the call.

It was Dr. Guttenberg back in Beverly Hills, apologizing for calling so late. The live-in therapist thought Fifer would want to know that his wife, Natalie, did not come home after her Pilates class. She was due to meet anniversary party planners at the house, but she never showed or called. Should they be concerned? Fifer made light of it, joking about Natalie's time management and that was that. He clicked off, knowing better than to share more. Of course he should be concerned. Hyung was more distrustful than ever since Fern pulled her stunt at the airport and let loose the Kim girl and the pool guy's kid. Natalie was no doubt an insurance policy. With the opening price of the stock already way up and the mega-profits singing in Hyung's head, Fifer had given his assurance that he would see the IPO launch through. In return he had gotten Hyung's assurance that he would leave his daughter, Fern, alone. Did he trust him? Fifer saw no other option. The Asian muscle took back the cell phone and gave the financier privacy once more. Fifer got into bed sick at heart, more frightened than he'd ever been. The truth hurt. He had no one to blame but his sorry, greedy self.

11.

right Now

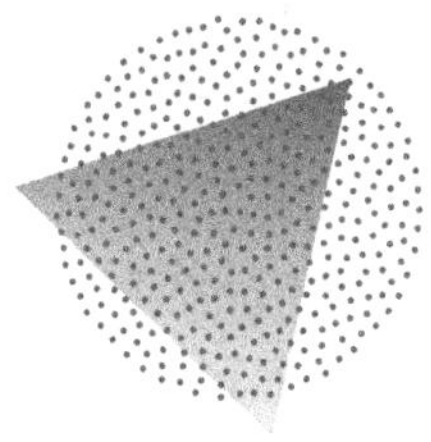

 Duke and Abby Jo go toward the front door. VJ and Leticia to the kitchen. Aeura, Fern, and I head to the rear. Before we reach the sliders that lead to the pool and the beach, we hear Duke yell.

There's a car blocking Fern's in the driveway. A black Lexus!

-It's Detective Boylan's. Lock the doors.

I whisper that as loud as possible. Using one knuckle, Duke gingerly double-locks it. VJ does the same in the kitchen. Fern secures the back sliders too. We can't miss the sight of a large man in a suit sitting on a pool chair outside. He waves to us. VJ and Leticia confirm another goon is stationed at the kitchen side of the house. We have been outmaneuvered and have locked ourselves in. We collect in the living room, our flashlights illuminating worried faces. VJ breaks the silence.

They could break in if they wanted to, but they don't. So we're safe here.

-Till they get what they want.

--and get to keep it.

---We are...

----The poop in the pool!

At once, everyone choruses in on that. Aeura laughs and it's catchy. A tension releaser. *A whistling passed the graveyard moment*, says Duke.

Leticia is pragmatic.

Could the Malibu police help? There's a number on the fridge.

-Could be in Boylan's pocket. Better we go to the press. I have friends. Say the word.

--Sorry AJ, but what real proof can we offer to turn this shit show around?

Abby Jo likes being challenged by Duke, and I see my old man give her a glance that if it isn't cute, it's sweet. Cute? Sweet? Duke? Abby Jo looks stunned. Very unlike Duke to lead on a lady. He is a firm believer in what you see is what you get with him—namely, red flag, bad boyfriend ahead. Oh boy. Not my business. Aeura pokes me with her elbow.

Tell them, Gilly. You have the TikTok video.

-And the voicemail from Owen, the bookstore clerk they killed.

With voicemail comment from VJ, I take a moment to feel the sting of guilt again. Aeura sees it and pulls me close in unconditional support. I like that. I wonder why all this love is coming to me now. Is it because no future is guaranteed? The heart leads in the void. My heart. I try to remember a Lorca poem about it. I feel Aeura's very soul. I want to kiss her and block everything else out. Leticia pulls us both into a huddle and whispers with heated breath into my ear.

Email that video and voicemail to yourself.

-Get it into the cloud, dude.

VJ's words are warm around our faces as he joins our illuminated trio. His flashlight dies, along with his phone's battery. Sweet. Not.

No internet here anyway.

-But if you could get down to the shore. Ah…

Aeura's right. My head is spinning. *Problem-solving is puzzle-solving,* my mom would say, pouring over her crosswords. The others check their phones' power.

I have over twenty percent charge. They can't stop our 5G. I'm calling my father!

-I have six percent. I'm calling home. Going to be late.

--Maybe your mom could call my folks. It's a school day tomorrow.

Good luck. No bars now. No signal. That's weird. We could get calls before.

Fern discovers like the others that we have no cell service. Apparently, they can stop 5G. Or is that coincidence too? People drift into their own heads, thinking the worst. I won't do that.

I need to use someone's cell. I'm going out. Duke… Duke?

I scan the darkened room and see two silhouettes in the corner shadows. Duke and Abby Jo are lip-locked and working it. Everyone sees what I see. VJ says it.

Get a room, kids!

-Okay. Where?

Duke is only too willing. I have other ideas.

Not now, Dad. We need you.

-Me?

Your particular set of skills. How are your hands?

-Smooth as a baby's…

That leaves everyone wondering.

 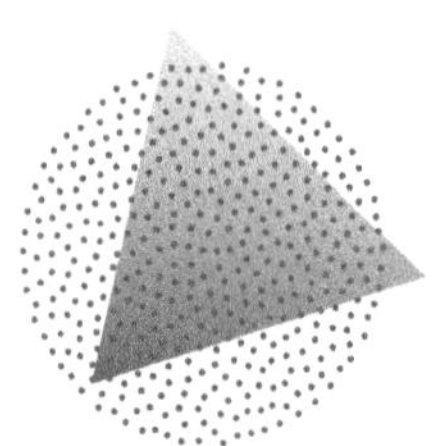

12.

Monday Night, five minutes Later

NOBODY CAN TWIRL A LONG POOL SKIMMER LIKE duke. Seriously, he could be on *America's Got Talent*. He actually tried out but blew off a callback audition to go to my mom's (his ex's) funeral. He won that day in my mind. I told my pop I needed him to distract the OG guarding the pool area so I could get down to the shore unseen. He was all in, gloves on and all. The big dummy with a gun didn't have a chance with Duke's opening charm offensive. The swarthy mountain of a man rose up at the sight of Duke coming outside. He puffed out his massive chest and patted a sidearm beneath his sport jacket to command Duke's attention.

Inside we all watched and listened from the back windows and sliders as Duke schmoozed the big guy with all he knew about Armenian women, courtesy of a girlfriend he once had from Yerevan, the capital. The Dukester had the man laughing and agreeing while he worked his way to a few skimmers lying poolside. A Swimline adjustable, one of Duke's absolute favorite models, caught his eye. He grabbed hold of the slender, six-foot, silver pole with the big turquoise dip net at the end. Before the guard could challenge it, Duke went into his top-shelf routine. Something like a baton twirler meets a Scottish caber-tosser meets Carrot Top is the only way to describe the performance. If it wasn't so dark, VJ's videoing would have done it justice. Duke brought his *A* game despite the ordeal he had suffered. What a champ! I was poised, on deck till Duke moved the mesmerized guard's sight line and I had my opening. Without hesitation I stepped out, moving with stealth around the pool for the shore. Out of sight, I snagged internet again at the water's edge.

With Fern's phone I logged myself in and got our evidence into the cloud—and into Leticia's and VJ's email. Do I feel I should have done that before? Ya! VJ would taunt me on such an amateur flub, but now it was out there in the ether ready to bring down the whole stinking plot. Thinking defense, I also emailed my cloud password to the only person I could trust who wasn't in as much danger as us. I'm sure when my cousin Ignacio—whom we call Nacho—in Santiago, Chile, wakes up and gets this, he will know what to do if I don't survive another night.

While Duke built to the dip-net-landing-on-his-head finish, I wound my way through the pockets of blackness back inside the open slider. The others crowded me. I felt hugs from Aeura, Leticia, Fern, and VJ, who all wanted to know why on earth I came back.

To get you all, of course. VJ, you parked on the highway, ya?

-Ya. West side. Why?

You can reach the road from a sand dune path down the beach.

--Ah yes. Very good, Gilly. But how do we all slip out without the guards noticing?

-Jailbreak? Full-on rush? Gilly?

I had nothing for them until Duke swaggered back in and was met with applause. No one was prouder of him than Abby Jo. Well, besides me. Duke beamed at the attention.

Godzilla was begging for more!

-Then we should give it to him.

An encore? Gilly, are you serious?

-Think Rosin bar mitzvah pool party.

Dad's smile of recognition gave me a shot of courage. I felt confident I could get everyone safely out—everyone, that is, but Duke and me.

gILLY

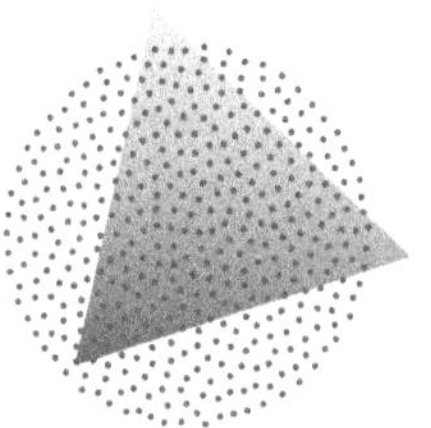

right Now

it's WAY, WAY, WAY After MidNight. We are in the dark in the beach house kitchen, but the light within us all shines. It's a group effort now. We have a plan with some wrinkles, and preparations have begun. Everyone is busy. I am helping mix up some pails of soapy water. VJ blindly scrounges in cabinets for a tool set. On a chair Leticia feels around upper shelves for whatever can be used. She gives a triumphant cry.

I got ant spray!

-I got brooms.

Abby Jo grabs what she can from a closet, brooms scattering. Aeura is off in a bathroom gathering spray bottles of perfume.

Someone's been smoking in here!

-My last one! Give me a break, doll!

VJ's voice rings out from the living room.

Eureka!

-Tools?

More booze! Bottles of Tito's!

That gets Abby Jo's attention. And Duke's.

Perfect conversation starter and gift.

-Alright. Everyone, bring it in here.

I call in the troops and we hang close. Those with flashlights use them. It does not feel spooky. It feels holy. I kick off the rundown.

Duke and I will occupy the pool guard so the girls can get out.

-I watch Boylan in the front.

VJ looks like a warrior with a hammer and screwdriver in hand.

Right. Then, when he's heading for the pool—

-Puncture his tires.

And take off for your car. Leticia—

-I hustle Aeura, Abby Jo, and Fern down the beach and up the path and meet VJ.

Aeura, Abby Jo, and Fern choose from an assortment of sprays, testing each. The air is pungent and Aeura, lightheaded, sprays me with perfume and kisses it.

Good luck, Gilly.

Leticia is not to be outdone and spray-plants a kiss.

Good luck.

VJ takes the moment to initiate some *good luck hugs* of his own with Leticia and Aeura. Abby Jo has gotten into the vodka and tries to smother Duke, but he cuts that short.

Hey, hey. You smell delicious. Later, AJ.

-Everyone okay with this? Fern, you are quiet.

Fern loads her pink revolver with purpose.

I'm not okay with this. I'm staying back with you and Duke.

-Then I am too.

--What? I'm not leaving.

---Look—either we all leave together, or we don't leave!

-For sure. Screw this "guys protecting girls" stuff.

Aeura looks inspired. Leticia committed. Fern, well, armed and dangerous. Abby Jo raises a clenched fist salute.

Girl power!

It is officially a mutiny. The great escape is going to have more moving parts.

I always see myself as a leader. I do not ever think others see me that way. So it has been easy for me to criticize leaders from afar, knowing I could do better. The comfort of the class ceiling. I accept I will never get a free ride to that kind of respect. There, I have said it. So… *#mysurprise.* I may have been wrong! Reading the room, the whole night in fact, everyone is waiting for what I think we should do next. Even Duke.

There's three of them, seven of us. Let's take a few and lay this out. Everybody, sit.

-Roger that, Gil! And good news, I think we have some Gladstones left.

Aeura checks the fridge. VJ is correct. She grabs the big platter.

Why not? Could be our last meal.

-Cold comfort food.

Leticia succinctly adds this observation. And with those happy thoughts we dig in and plot.

tueſday, 6:45 a.m.
eaſtern time

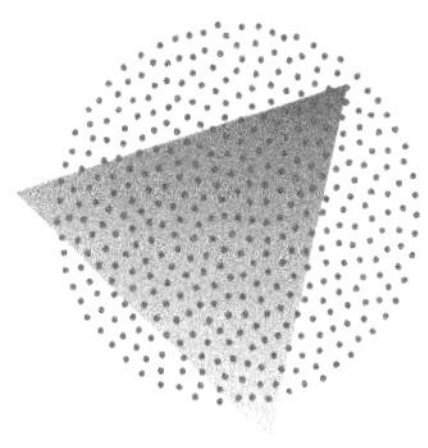

 She told him her captors were treating her well. The mattress is too soft and the bedspring squeaks, but she has cable TV with HBO in the locked bedroom. She had Philip laughing about the so-called dinner and her aversion to the taste of *topik*, Armenian chickpea dumplings. He told her to hold on a little longer. It was all smooth sailing and would be over by the opening bell. He told her she could watch live on any business channel.

He kept it positive with her. It was not hard. He wanted to believe it. Money soothes most problems. In this case there was such a windfall that it paid for all to be on their best behavior. He knew Hyung understood that. He hoped the Armenian mob did.

With Rodney Allan out of the equation, they seemed to have no one controlling them. Fifer made Hyung promise him that Fern would be okay till he returned. She was being isolated in a house in Malibu with her friends. A Beverly Hills police detective was in charge, not the Armenians. Hyung repeated that to emphasize the point. Fifer had also just spoken with his loyal Beverly Hills office manager, Thomas Shephard. To think, the week before, the young go-getter was nearly fired by the duplicitous Brad. Fifer wondered how much Hyung had promised Brad, Fifer's once-trusted assistant.

Shep was a new Fifer favorite. The kid, a USC grad, had smartly arranged for a live feed with all the finbiz cablers. It would showcase the opening bell party at the West Coast office for the small cadre of employees, each of whom Phil looked after like an old-school boss. It was a life-changing event for them, and it was newsworthy. The staffers themselves would become rich. He was glad for that. His sacrifice would be appreciated and honored by all he had touched. He would even forgive Fern. Clearly the pool guy's kid was a bad influence. Fifer made a mental note to email Duke and terminate the service.

The financial maven of Beverly Hills dressed in his finest and was amazed to be feeling so pleased about the veneration to come. In the bathroom mirror he saw the sinister, rough piece of hired muscle looming, studying his every move, snapping Fifer back to a grimmer reality.

* * *

The night before, at Peter Luger Steak House, Tomoko Kim had endured a dinner with James Hyung and his twin daughters. They had flown into New York to join their beloved dad for the momentous occasion. Hyung did not miss an opportunity to praise his own parenting and make Tomoko feel even worse for raising a rebellious daughter. At their after-dinner goodnight exchange it got worse. He was curt to her in front of his children and left her feeling insulted. She made up her mind to not be so compliant in the future. She and Aeura deserved their money, and like Fifer she had been guaranteed her daughter would not be harmed in any way. She cursed that pool boy for befriending Aeura and clouding her mind. Aeura would understand in time. Tomoko would set up a trust fund for her. The divorcée from Houston knew she had a few good years left herself and didn't want to worry about having enough savings. If she had to do something of which she was ashamed, she could live with that. The unforeseen suicide of her ex-husband, Sidney Kim, was to blame, and part of her wished she had her daughter's courage to challenge it. If he was not a murderer but a victim, Aeura and she would be getting what they deserved—Sidney's lion's share of the IPO. Instead, Tomoko had to promise silence, debasing herself in her daughter's name for a tenth of what they were owed.

Her hotel wake-up call came at 7 a.m., but Tomoko had not slept at all. She showered, dried, and pampered, lost in thought. Before dressing for the Wall Street event, she suddenly felt unclean. Despite the risk of being late and upsetting Hyung, Tomoko stepped back once more into a steamy shower of regret.

* * *

Alone in the big house in the flats of Beverly Hills, Dr. Guttenberg had not gone to bed, though it was after 4 a.m. on the West Coast. He was troubled by his inability to reach Fern or Detective Boylan. Dr. Guttenberg knew his live-in position with the Fifers was nothing more than being Fern's manny to keep her productive. This whole sordid business with the pool guy's kid was an epic mistake he never should have indulged. He was the prime enabler and fretted it could be a tipping point for his dismissal. Pushing seventy-nine, Dr. Guttenberg did not relish going back into the job market or attempting to hang a shingle. Suspecting his best bet was with Fern, he filled a Yeti with Perrier, grabbed the keys to his orange Kia, and headed off into the dead of night.

* * *

From her lonely king-sized bed on the second floor of her Westwood house, Professor Bethany Almora couldn't stop listening for the front door to open and close. A few hours earlier she had been woken from a CBD-induced slumber by the panicked parents of a classmate of her daughter, Leticia. VJ's mother and father, each on their own phone, apologized for calling so late. The professor had her classes in the morning and had gone to bed early. Groggy, she was not much help to them. Their son had not come home either and was not answering his phone. VJ's parents asked her if she was worried. She was hazy for sure but still said no. She had faith in Leticia's decision-making. That was during the eleven o'clock nightly news. It was now 4:17 a.m., and Bethany was having second and third thoughts. Leticia should have been in by midnight. When VJ's parents called, his mother said she had been calling hospitals, fearing they were in some wreck. Before hanging up, VJ's father had relayed that he believed the unexplained behavior was about the Jacuzzi Murder business that the damn Gilly Montrose had dragged VJ into. Professor Almora had thanked him and promised to call back if she heard anything.

Bethany, in need of sleep, any sleep, and jet-lagged from her Costa Rican fling, now doubled the dosage of CBD droplets. Though she was worried deep in her heart, she trusted her daughter enough that she finally passed out again, with one ringing thought—this Gilly, the pool guy's kid, was bad news.

right Now

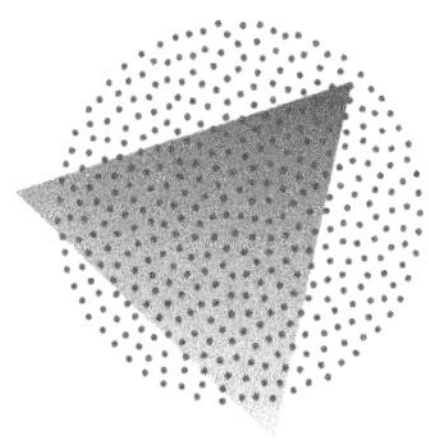

 hitting the shore in a monotonous metronome, counting us down. One *crash*, two *crash*, three. We are ready. It's on!

Duke has an unopened bottle of Tito's and steps out the back slider. The pool area is now illuminated by tiki torches. The behemoth guard in the suit is reading a foreign language newspaper beneath a flaming torch. Not rising from his deck chair, he lets his booming voice do the job. Through his thick accent the words are still clear.

Get your ass inside.

-What!? Buddy! I wrestled this bottle from the kids for you.

Duke flashes it. That gets the big man's attention. He yawns and points to a poolside table. Duke sets it down with two red Solo cups. I am watching from the laundry room window and can no longer hear what is being said. The guard cracks open the bottle and pours for Duke and himself. There is joking between them, alongside the drinking. Duke can handle his vodka, but now he is nursing his cup as I suggested (and he pooh-poohed!). It seems to be taking longer than it should. I calm the others and we stay patient.

Duke stands and with blue-gloved hands grabs the two skimmer poles up against the pump shed. He hands one to the guard. Standing up, the guard grins with curiosity. He tries twirling it himself. His suit jacket flaps, and his shoulder holster gets in the way. As I strain my eyes to see, the thug removes the holster and places it on the table—something we never, ever imagined. He takes another drink. Duke is surging with adrenalin and sneaks a look back to the house, which he knows I see. He has the guard under his tutelage and gives a lesson. The guard is focused and works the pole, with Duke's encouragement. He has some talent, and I wonder if I should get myself out there. But the guy is feeling the liquor, and the pole goes flying onto the sand. He laughs, and the Dukester holds up a hand and hurries back to the house. He slips in through the sliding door and takes a breath.

Okay, the bait's on the hook. Let's rock and reel!

I signal to the others, and they move quietly in the darkened house to their stations like a midnight army. Duke pats my cheek and musses up my scalp so it resembles bed hair. I have hold of two buckets of soapy water. Duke has us wait another minute. In that minute he tells me how much he loves me. They are words I have never heard from him. I have felt them, but it's like I never expected him to bother uttering them. Not his style. I nod with chest swelling. He drags me outside and announces to the guard.

Joseph! Fresh from dreamland, my son.

-C'mon, Dad. I don't want to do this.

I promised Joseph something special.

Duke slurs words, playing the drunk, gathering both poles. I whine, doing my part. Duke fits the buckets on a pool skimmer like weights on a barbell. He hands it to me with an un-Duke-like sternness.

Hey, screwup. Do something right.

I curse under my breath at dear old Dad, and he returns to Joseph the guard.

Joseph. Okay, name a favorite song?

-"Ara Vay."

Uh, I don't know that one, but could you sing or hum a little to give us a beat?

Tipsy, Joseph the guard stomps in time and gives voice to the Armenian pop tune. Duke directs him where he wants him to stand for the best view. With a flourish Duke starts twirling his skimmer across from me. On the other side of the pool I start lifting the skimmer up and down like a weight lifter with rhythm. Three lifts in and on the fourth I steady it, holding it over my head. Duke lets loose his twirling skimmer. It soars and rotates through the air over the width of the pool, coming my way. I track it and thrust up, bouncing it off the pole above my head. I direct it right back across the pool to Duke. He catches it with precision and twirls into it without losing the cadence. We have practiced this during many bored hours and have performed it for special clients and pool events. We do another round of it, and I bop his skimmer higher. It pinwheels back, and Duke does a twirl himself before snagging the sucker behind his back! The good-time guard applauds. Duke maneuvers next to the guard and takes a bow.

Now this you gotta see. Gilly—

-No! I'm not gonna do it. Too wasted. I'll miss.

Do it. Throw it!

I am exhausted and wish I did have a shot of coffee. Concentration wins out. I stretch my fingers, regrip, and nod to Duke. He sets his feet. I let it go with a mighty heave and my best aim. Usually, we fill the buckets with confetti right before and the bar mitzvah boy thinks it's water and gets a good surprise. But occasionally in an adult show it is water.

Water gives it weight. My toss arcs high above the water and drops down fast—not on Dad but on the guard. Instinctively his hands go up and he tries to catch it. No way. It crashes on him. The soapy brew sloshes over. Off-balance in more ways than one the big man fights for traction, and his feet slip on the wet surface. As the WWE commentators explain every week on TV, *"Once you compromise a man's vertical base, he is history."* Duke swings his skimmer pole hard behind Joseph's knees, and the goon crumbles with an angry howl, tumbling forward into the pool at the deep end.

His cry brings his reinforcements running. Boylan leaves his car at the driveway. The muscle man at the side door leaves his post. There is only one direct way for them to get to the pool. Through the dark house—the *locked* dark house.

I give Duke enough time to grab the holstered pistol, keeping the big man under with a metal pole end pushed into his submerged mass. I lean my weight into it, and it feels good. It's a release to strike back, and I scare myself for a moment before I ease up. The guard coming to the surface thrashes out to snatch the pole from my hands, but I pull it away—it's not necessary with Duke holding Joseph's .45 Automatic and pointing at him.

Now, this is entertaining. Well done, son.

--Thanks, Dad.

---I will rip your hearts out!

He spits those words. I wave out the others while the big man treads water, contemplating moves. He sees our forces surrounding him on the deck—Leticia with ant spray, Aeura with an extension cord whip, Fern with the pink gun locked and loaded. If this image got posted it would go viral, I am sure. With a small Tide detergent bottle tucked under her arm and a toothpick between her lips, Abby Jo pulls out a garden hose from the side of the house.

Turn it on and dump!

Abby Jo wets down the poolside's flagstone deck with water and the detergent. At the other side of the house at the front door Boylan and the other gangster have gathered. Their knocks become more forceful. VJ inside does not open it. In a dead zone of communication their raw yells cut through to the back of the property.

Joe! Joseph!

-You okay?

--No! I can't swim! Watch out! They have—

Before he can say more I *whap* the netted basket of the pool skimmer over his head and mute the words. Duke uses his pole net to douse the tiki lights. Darkness is our friend, and into the shadows we creep.

VJ, let them through!

He unlocks the front door and takes cover. The panicked Boylan and swarthy sidekick rush through the house, flashlights leading the way to the rear. Hurrying out the open back sliders into the black of night, they hit the slick surface and lose traction, feet flapping fast, like you see in cartoons. Wavering like towers of jelly, they slide across the deck, out of control, and splash into the pool. Plop. Plop. I swear this is true.

Only a pool guy appreciates the power of a slippery stone deck.

tuesday, 8:45 a.m.
eastern time

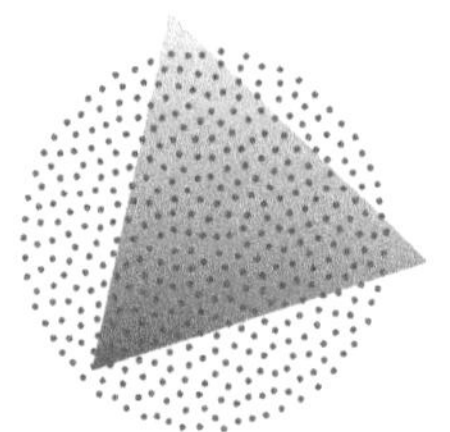

HYUNG CHEWED AT HIS NAILS, RUINING A PERFECT MANICURE. Dressed in a $20K Kiton cashmere suit he was coming out of his skin with frustration. Their limo had to wait for Tomoko and now was in gridlock traffic on South Broadway, en route to the New York Stock Exchange only a few blocks away. Tomoko Kim and Philip Fifer, also dressed to impress, shared the stretch with Hyung and tried to bear his discomfort. The lavish media celebration that was planned before the opening bell was going on without him, the star, and Hyung was not taking it well. Fifer reminded him that there was a West Coast event also planned at his Beverly Hills office, and the national business cablers had agreed to carry it live on both coasts after the opening. He was a firm believer that the first sixty minutes were paramount in propelling a new stock to its high through the trading day.

That's the golden hour when perception is forged.

Hyung appreciated that tip.

Yes. Brad alerted me to your office's live feed. He'll be there. I made sure.

Fifer took that on the chin. Hyung calmed as the traffic snarl gave way to movement. They were close. Fifer hoped that Hyung was in touch with the detective. He expected his wife, Natalie, along with Fern and the others, to be released soon. Fifer and Tomoko had both tried unsuccessfully to reach their kids. Tomoko kept her head low.

They are not answering. No service, it seems.

A block away from Wall Street, Hyung, filling up with grandeur and a smidgen of gratitude, explained that a minority partner took the initiative and expense to disable a Malibu cell tower for the night.

To ensure the children's silence at this critical time.

-Of course. And that time is almost up.

Fifer pushed that point again. Hyung pushed back. He and the Beverly Hills detective had satellite phones for communication. As Phil Fifer and Tomoko watched, Hyung made a show of using it.

Let's get a boots-on-the-ground report. I want happy faces.

The billionaire-to-be punched in Boylan's number and let it ring. And ring. No one answered. In the limo an uncomfortable silence ensued.

* * *

On the West Coast the sun was creeping over a notch in the Malibu mountains at the county line. Dr. Guttenberg parked on the road by Fern's mother's beach house just after 6 a.m. Pacific Time. The front door was wide open, and there was a black Lexus with flat tires blocking the driveway sideways. He was not a brave man, but he stepped up to the portal despite this fact and peeked into the darkness of the home's interior. His voice cracked.

Fern?

-Help! Help! Help!

A panicked, muffled chorus of men's voices erupted from the rear. The old doctor threaded his way to the gaping sliding doors that led to the deck area. The first rays of morning light were across the pool. In the mist of dawn it was a sight to behold. Three grown men lashed together on their backs, shivering like inverted turtles on a tethered raft of pool skimmer poles buoyed by plastic chairs. Their mouths wrapped in Scotch tape did not prevent them from cursing at the old guy to hurry and get them the hell out. Dr. Guttenberg was an eternal student of human nature and betrayed a smirk, sensing the hand of the kids in this wicked floating tableau. The guardians undone by the guarded. The Beverly

Hills therapist was also an eternal wannabe screenwriter, and all the scenarios he could concoct told him one thing: leave. And without a word, that's what he did.

riɡHt Now

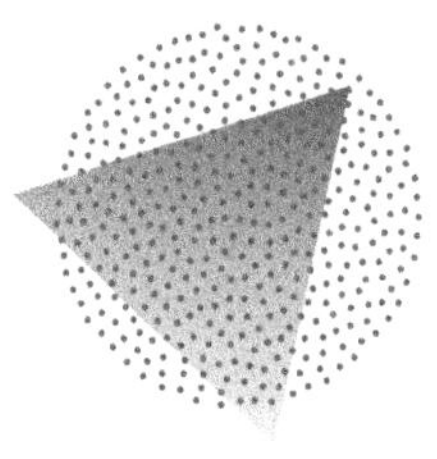

WE ARE BUMPING DOWN THE PACIFIC COAST HIGHWAY IN AN OVERLOADED OLD PRIUS.

Slow down!

-I'm not even going forty!

You're tailgating.

Duke is all over the driver. When you live on the Malibu shore, there is only one road in and the same road out—the Pacific Coast Highway. Even at this early hour there is fast-moving traffic heading south into the city. Heading north, nothing,

Duke hates this road. He calls it *Blood Alley.*

Guys, anyone see that orange Kia going the other way a few minutes ago?

-You think we can actually move our necks?

I think it was my therapist.

--If he's coming to our rescue, he's a little late.

We are seven crammed in VJ's car. VJ drives, and Duke has the front seat with Abby Jo on his lap. I am in the middle of the back seat with Fern and Leticia on either side and Aeura in my lap. We are free. I am hoping Duke doesn't spoil the sweet relief we are feeling by listing the number of notable folks who have died in car accidents on this legendary stretch of asphalt.

You know the movie, Romancing the Stone. Writer died right there. Director, A Christmas Story. I could go on.

-Don't.

Leticia squirms with discomfort.

This door handle is embedded in my thigh! We should have taken Boylan's car.

-Steal a police car, beautiful. That goes on your high school record.

Hey, VJ! I ant-sprayed the eyes of that detective. How much worse can it be?

--Truth will come out. Let's keep to the plan. Fern, we are depending on you.

---So is my dad.

----Stop the car! Let us out.

Duke is serious. VJ pulls over. I see the Reel Inn, a funky restaurant and motel across the highway, where I have enjoyed some Great Taco Tuesdays over the years. Duke has a friend who owns it, and he is out the door. He and Abby Jo give goodbyes.

You guys need some room. Don't worry about us.

-Us? I like the sound of that, Dukie boy.

Abby Jo's face goes from question mark to tickled. Duke is getting in deeper with her. I know Duke and it will not end well, but as my mom used to say with a shrug of a shoulder, "Toujours gai, toujours gai." Always happy, always happy.

Before getting back on the road, VJ pats the vacated front seat.

Who's coming up to sit?

The three girls who cling to me do not look anxious to move. I feel their attraction and it is unexpected and thrilling. Duke used to tell me to have faith with the opposite sex. *"You never think you are as cool and attractive as you really are."* I thought he was just speaking about himself. The stalemate breaks. Aeura leaves me first, gets out of the back seat and into the passenger seat next to VJ. Her smile at him makes it all go right. He puts it in gear and we are off. Leticia and Fern, with room to spare, still hug close and their warmth is measurable.

Let's get ready to kick some crypto BH butt!

Fern's declaration proves her to be a winner in the entitled genes department.

Hard to stop my sudden attraction to this young woman whom I'd previously considered a future Beverly Hills Stepford wife. Fern is so much more. Not even counting the money thing, she's a complete package. I mean, Leticia and Aeura are too. The wonder of these women. They are as beautiful and powerful as superheroes to me. If I was lucky enough to choose, I couldn't lose. Aeura is wild of spirit and has a poetic heart. Leticia is quality and the best kisser. Fern is a surprise a minute, but maybe too beautiful for me to go the distance. Am I tipping my hand? I hope this delicious agony never ends.

Of course it will. We are going to out ourselves and expose the murdering mf'ers, and if all goes to plan we will deliver justice. That sounds way pretentious—not to mention perhaps impossible. Rolling past Gladstones, nerves start to sink in. I have to ask VJ.

Can you really hack into a broadcast?

-Watch me.

In the rearview mirror, I see Aeura's face light up at his confidence. I feel surprisingly pleased for both. Three girls are a two-boy job. VJ turns off the Pacific Coast Highway at Sunset and heads east.

Where to?

-Wilshire and Rodeo.

--Phat City.

-Damn right. And step on it. Don't want to be late!

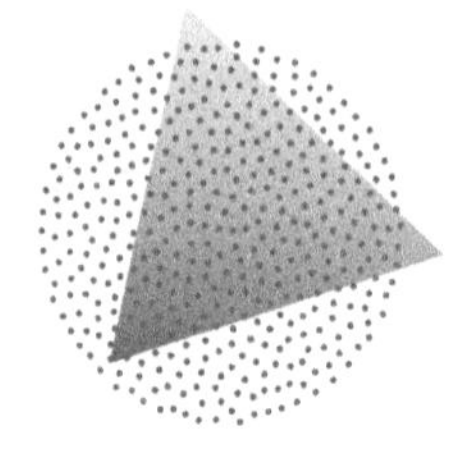

tuesday, 9:27 a.m. eastern time

it was three minutes till the stock market opened, and the Wall Street trading floor was a buzz of hysteria. The presale price for the Crypto Mining League IPO had rocketed up—and the projected profits to major shareholders along with it. Hyung was settled in a suite overlooking the trading floor, hosting company colleagues, his twins, and financial industry glad-handers waiting for the big bell to ring in the trading day, as is the tradition. News reporters and a few security personnel mingled, sampling the great buffet. The choice of bell ringer had been granted to Hyung—a privilege that Fifer's clout had garnered. On the recommendation of his daughters, Hyung chose an Instagram influencer, who was adding a surreal atmosphere to the normally staid institution. The Korean performance artist Jelly Chu, in an outrageous paper dress made of fake stock certificates, was posing provocatively for the cameras. A handler cued her, and the rainbow-haired young celeb excused herself to all, making a dramatic exit to tend to her duty.

Phil Fifer has been in this suite before. The "Winners' Circle," they called it. The adrenaline rush to an IPO's debut was usually intoxicating. Not today. Never had he felt more unease and—let's face it—disgust. He considered himself a gentleman who occasionally bent the rules because he had earned the right. Okay, inherited it. He knew Hyung was as evil as the gangsters that they were partnered with. How long could he pretend to believe that Rodney Allan and Sidney Kim's deaths were suicides? He'd skirted dirty deals a few times before but never with stone-cold killers under the umbrella of law enforcement.

Boylan was a tool of the Glendale boys, but did it stop with him? Fifer had a friend with the FBI he could still call. But his investors' trust and their money weighed on his mind. At least that's what he kept telling himself. Besides, he dared not stop playing along for fear of endangering his wife and daughter. He knew Tomoko Kim was in the same complicated boat. Their legal exposure, should the truth ever come out, spelled ruin for anyone connected. Worse, that threat would always make him and Tomoko a liability to their conniving partners. He looked around for Tomoko. She was not in the suite. Fifer caught the eye of Hyung. He was savoring the spotlight but took the moment and joined Fifer with a clap on the back. Hyung had brought this IPO to market by hook and by crook. The ends always justified the means. Though not a religious man, Hyung gave a silent prayer to God for good fortune and pulled the Beverly Hills moneyman in close, feeling the grand prize in his hand.

We did it!

Fifer felt smothered. The time had come. With a flourish, Jelly Chu rang the big brass bell. The market opened!

At 6:30 a.m. Pacific Time, a mighty cheer for the start of trading day went up from within the Fifer Family Financial Fund building on Rodeo and Wilshire in the heart of Beverly Hills. The partying was so loud and exuberant it could be heard outside the two-story Spanish Colonial office building as VJ's Prius with Gilly and company pulled up. They drove right by the two TV trucks doubled-parked by the entry door with its gleaming gold plaque, "FFFF, Established 1932." They turned into the private garage entrance of Fern's father, the firm's president. Fern knew the entry code for the gate, and VJ parked in Mr. Fifer's spot, right by the direct access door to his office. Before getting out of the car, I put my hand up like at a debate team match. One by one, Aeura, VJ, Leticia, and Fern—all in—clasped their hands to mine.

It was now or never.

7.

rigHt NoW

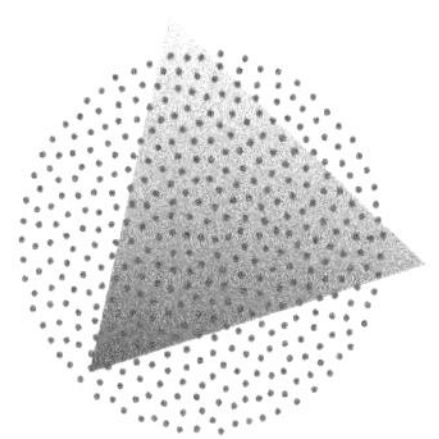

 No one knows we are here. We can hear whoops and hollers from the main office beyond our walls every time the stock price goes up—which is nonstop. The market has been open for five minutes, and we are watching it unfold on a big TV screen tuned to a muted business-news channel. Peeking through curtains at the crowded bullpen area inside, I can see thirty or forty people celebrating amid two roving cable news cameras covering the office party. A cookie-cutter blonde on-air reporter is interviewing a Fifer Family

Financial Fund employee. Behind them by the punch bowl I spot a well-dressed, elated duo that I recognize too well. The killer, Hartunian, is laughing with asshat Brad from the airport. Oh well.

I join my little group, standing around a big antique desk. Fern helps VJ sign in to her father's desktop PC. Online, he gets his mojo working.

Yes! They're pivoting off a public platform. No patches. No firewall. It was harder to break into Pokemon GO.

-Asian ingenuity!

Aeura is pumped and kisses VJ on the cheek. Fern and Leticia will not be outdone. VJ is genuinely embarrassed.

I know I am your stereotypical IT guy.

-But cuter.

--Way.

---Stay in your lane, bro.

----Always good advice.

Thank you. We have camera and audio. Standing by.

VJ adjusts a plug-and-play HD camera snapped onto the desktop's monitor. He gets out of the seat.

Fern, it's all yours.

-My mother always says I could be a news anchor. I hope she's watching.

Fern settles into her father's black leather desk chair and primps her hair, using the monitor as mirror. She looks world-class. Ready to get the show on the road, VJ stands, holding the keyboard like a rock star. Leticia has no hard copy to distribute, so she beats the rundown into us. We have some options in this plan of attack but don't have much time.

Gilly, once you're out the door, find the cameras. That's the money. Fern will introduce you.

-Got it.

Aeura nods along with every reminder from Leticia, who is all business. Everything I have ever felt for Leticia was so spot-on. She is a phenomenon. Aeura, too, is a beautiful beating heart of soul, and I have such love for her. She always looks hip and ready in her black leather jacket. I feel suddenly inadequate. A final costume adjustment from Mr. Fifer's coat rack and, with a $500 plaid scarf around my neck and everyone's approval, I open the door to the main office. Aeura and I step into the party.

 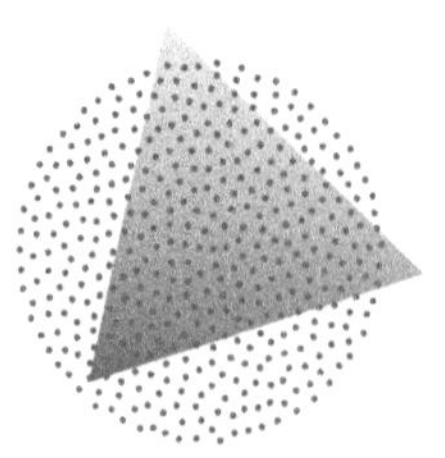

one minute later,
new york city

phil fifer was on the phone with his wife, natalie, getting her ready for freedom, when he noticed Hyung's sudden mood swing. The Korean mastermind finished a phone call and stormed over to Fifer, who was still on his cell.

Hold on a sec. What's wrong, James?

-Tomoko Kim's daughter and that pool boy just crashed your office party!

What?! Have Brad get rid of them!

-Yes, and the police will help too! Your daughter's safety guarantee has expired!

Across the suite, a very pleased stock exchange biggie waved for Hyung to join his excited twin daughters who were posing with the official and the Instagram influencer. Hyung headed over, brows furrowed and teeth clenched. Fifer got back on the phone to Natalie, speaking firmly but in a soft voice.

Can you get out of the house?

-I think so. They're out in the backyard having breakfast.

Go!

-Phil! I haven't finished my makeup.

Fifer didn't respond to that inanity. On the big HD monitor in the Wall Street exchange suite, cable news was showing his Beverly Hills office party. Abruptly the broadcast began to shimmy with static. The TV image was replaced by Fifer's daughter, Fern. Her face filled the eighty-inch, hi-def screen like a professional newscaster. VJ had hacked the broadcast. A *Breaking News* chyron banner, courtesy of our man on the keyboard, scrolled beneath her, followed by the words: *Murderers revealed…* Fifer was flush with panic. Fern was in his office, in his chair!

Hi, I'm Fern Fifer. Welcome, everyone, to our firm's IPO party.

right now

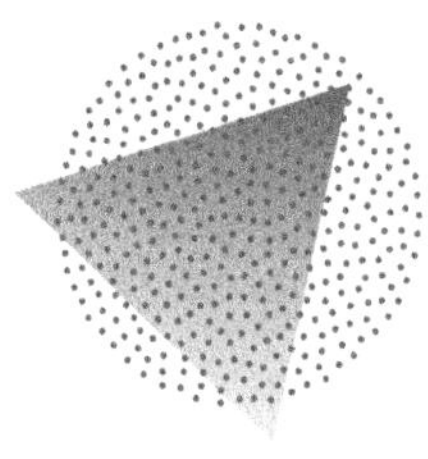

with Aeura's hand in mine, I weave her through the jubilant, partying crowd of instant millionaires who have not yet caught on to what's just happened. That's how smooth Fern is as a talking head. Brad and Hartunian are more than aware, and they are coming right for us. I push through toward the closest TV reporter as Fern's live image on all the TVs cues us.

Everyone, please welcome special guests Aeura Kim, daughter of the accused Jacuzzi Murderer, and Gilly Montrose, who was also once accused. Hi, Aeura! Hi, Gilly! Over to you. Who done it, kids?

VJ hits a few keystrokes and switches the broadcast back to the cable news feed in time for the excited on-camera reporters to pepper me and Aeura with questions. As Leticia predicted, Hartunian is paralyzed to stop us on live TV. Instead, he signals Brad off toward the source of the broadcast—Fifer's office. Aeura faces the cameras and delivers our prepared statement.

My father did not kill his wife or himself. Nor are he and Mr. Philip Fifer responsible for the three other deaths that cloud this company's stock offering. It is an IPO that is covered in blood.

-What? Three deaths? Who is behind them? Name names!

The reporters are foaming. They are on the verge of real news, high-crime news. The room hushes. The partygoers, frozen with sudden concern, focus on us under the harsh TV lights. Aeura hesitates. Like me she sees Hartunian's hand move under his jacket. She is not afraid and nails it.

The murderers are company CEO James Hyung, assisted by members of a Glendale criminal gang under the protection of certain individuals in the Beverly Hills Police Department.

The two stunned on-air reporters volley back from both sides.

That's quite an accusation!

-You have proof?

--Yes, we have proof! We are proof!

---Fern! Get out!

I yell that into the camera, seeing Brad and security personnel at Fern's father's office door. Alerted inside, Fern guides Leticia and VJ out the back and into the garage. Brad and the guards smash at the locked private entrance doors to Fifer's office, and commotion is in motion. The cable broadcast is over. Hartunian inches closer, hand inside his jacket. His gun slides out. Two uniformed Beverly Hills cops join him on either side. I am so scared that I can't control myself. I scream.

Active shooter!!!

That tears it. It's chaos at the Fifer Family Financial Fund IPO party. Some run. Others duck and cover. Aeura and I aim for the big front doors, in a stampeding crowd of frightened celebrants. I look back and see Hartunian and the cops stalled by the confused, escaping throng.

Outside I jaywalk Aeura across the street in the heart of the city, already bustling at 7 a.m. We don't look back. South of the boulevard, I hurry her along. She's with me step by step.

We're good. I know a safe place.

-Of course you do. I love you, Gilly.

That hits me hard. I can't form words. I stare at her instead, mouth agape. Aeura laughs and tugs at my arm.

You dope! C'mon!

I am a dope, an overwhelmed one. Leticia and Aeura have both told me they love me in the last twenty-four hours. The morning is brightening.

tuesday, 10:02 a.m. eastern time

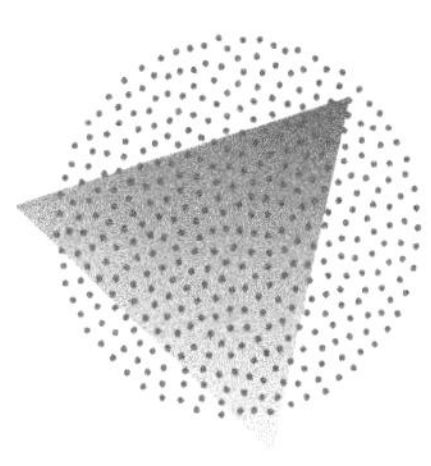

it was darkening with doom at the wall street stock exchange and at brokerage houses across the world. The IPO darling of the day, the Crypto Mining League, was sinking like a stone, with investor uncertainty and fear for the company's future. The frenetic free-fall run of sell orders was mercifully curtailed when it was announced that its trading had been halted, effectively killing its prospects. In the joyless suite Hyung was alternating between two cell phones, screaming into both, trying to control the damage and wreak vengeance. Hyung's twins were crying and asking him questions he did not want to answer. The Instagram influencer in her stock certificate dress crossed her arms and avoided Hyung like the plague, tiptoeing her way out. Hyung was devasted by the turn. Searching the room, he realized his partners were nowhere in sight. The Korean businessman, momentary billionaire, and murderous human abandoned his children and fled the suite alone.

Hyung didn't get far. At the Wall Street entrance, he was stopped for questioning on the sidewalk by two plainclothes FBI men. The agency had been tipped off from both coasts no less than four times since sunup. Two of the whistleblowers had criminal exposure themselves, falling on their swords, making it all the more believable and urgent.

Tomoko and Fifer had made calls, as did Abby Jo and Dr. Guttenberg. The hack of the Beverly Hills IPO party's broadcast and the on-camera accusations by Aeura and Gilly could not be unseen or unheard. Hyung pleaded his case to the federal agents and an arriving U.S. Marshal from a white-collar task force assigned to the district. Hyung floated a bribe a second. The lawmen did not budge and he was led off. It was a perp walk captured live by business-news cameras for all to see. He passed Fifer and Tomoko in custody as well. They glared at Hyung with something beyond hatred, enjoying his pain more than suffering their own misfortune.

* * *

Duke and Abby Jo were holed up in a borrowed bedroom at the Reel Inn on the Pacific Coast Highway. He did not have to be reminded that she had saved his life, and he swore his gratitude. Under the sheets they toasted with plastic cups of vodka to the video images of Hyung's arrest. It was sweet to see it, and they were so impressed with these kids. Abby Jo kissed Duke with tenderness.

You're a good father.

Duke appreciated that. Or seemed to. At a commercial break on the TV, Abby Jo went to take a long, hot shower, and Duke did the most Duke thing. Whether it was her compliment that triggered him or the thought of domesticity in general, he dressed, wrote a short note to Abby Jo explaining he had to work, dropped a few twenties next to the note, and hightailed it into the wind. The old French exit, Irish goodbye, or in this case, the *El Duque adios*. Abby Jo should have seen it coming.

* * *

After busting out of the Fifer building's private garage in VJ's car, Leticia kept them focused on their first option. They dropped Fern off at Beverly Hills High in time for school, and Leticia and VJ made it to Uni High before the first period bell. In the corridor Leticia kept looking over her shoulder for police or worse. VJ calmed her. It was all over Twitter already. The IPO disaster and arrest of its CEO was trending. He whispered.

We crushed it.

-We did.

VJ was almost as tall as Gilly, and Leticia looked up at him with fresh eyes and a reborn spirit. They hugged deeply, bodies pressed with an intimacy beyond that of comrades in arms.

Despite the hordes of gawking classmates passing by them, their eyes were on each other. They had never been closer. VJ broke the moment, stricken with thought.

It's weird Aeura and Gilly haven't checked in.

-Maybe they didn't get away.

That thought struck Leticia. VJ assured Leticia they did. He had seen Gilly and Aeura in his rearview mirror outside the Fifer building.

Gilly will stick to the plan. Lots of places for them to hide, pools we've worked nearby.

Leticia felt better. Not really. The thought of Gilly and Aeura alone suddenly bothered her. It further bothered the competitive, debate club leader that it did bother her, considering that she was not bothered at all in the loving warmth of VJ's arms.

Leticia, is something bothering you?

-No, nothing.

right now

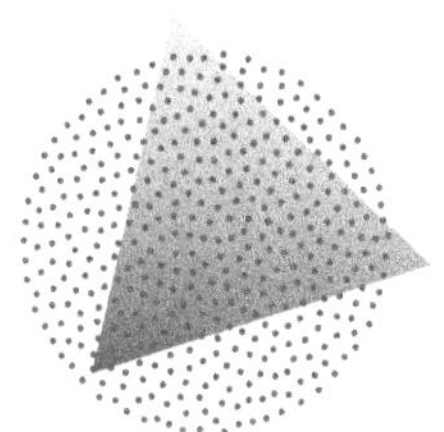

our shoes are off, and we sit poolside with our feet dangling in the water. It's cold, to be sure, winter in LA, and the small pool is unheated. But the sun is warm on our faces, and without phones we are clueless about what has transpired since we fled the Fifer Family Financial Fund office. Aeura is shoulder to shoulder with me, and we have not spoken a word in a while. It's wonderful. Finally, she speaks.

This place is a dump.

-Yes, but I love it.

Hidden by larger single-family houses off El Camino and Charleville Boulevard, I have taken Aeura to a '40s Spanish-style apartment triplex and its well-maintained period pool. With the gate code embedded in my memory, I have sequestered us for safety's sake within its enclosed backyard. Let time breathe. The three apartments are unoccupied and have been for the last two years, tied up in probate court. The owners, Mrs. Ziegler and her family, have been friends of mine since my mother and I moved in after she and Duke divorced.

I learned to swim in this pool.

-Is it clean?

For sure! It's serviced once a month.

I do it for nothing as a favor to the family. It keeps me in touch with memories of my mom too. We had so many Christmases here, so many Easter hams. Mom was a very good cook. My feet are ice and I raise them, shaking off the water right onto Aeura.

We should go in.

-What? It's freezing. Gotta be below fifty-five degrees. California zero.

Aeura is pushing for this and I am a willing enabler. She starts losing outer garments first and I follow because, wouldn't you? We strip down to our underwear and steel ourselves to plunge in. I see a firebird rising from the ashes tattooed on Aeura's back.

It's a phoenix.

-I know. It's very...you.

You have no tattoos.

-Nope. Promised my mom.

I defied mine. Things will never be the same between us now, you know?

-That's a good thing. Maybe?

Aeura connects with that thought. She declares she's learned one sure thing from this ordeal: she is not going to college. She dreams of being a writer and wants to see the world to fill in the words she will need. I like that notion. Or am I just delaying jumping into the frigid blue? Aeura delays too.

That's always been my dream.

-"Don't give up on your dreams, or your dreams will give up on you."

Yes, good one.

-It's a saying from a famous UCLA basketball coach Duke has been known to quote a lot.

I felt obligated to share some great John Wooden wisdom as we put immersion on pause.

"Be quick, never hurry."

-I agree.

"Make every day your masterpiece."

-I'm down.

"Adversity doesn't make character, it reveals it."

-Nothing more adverse than this freezing water, Gilly!

With that she pushes me in and cannonballs right after.

Awwww!

It's a delicious shock to the system. We both surface, survive, and adapt. Game on as to who can stay in longer.

Our teeth chatter, and like all mammals seeking warmth we cling to each other. The glistening, exquisite pool water is a sensual adhesive bonding us, skin on skin. We cannot break this embrace. Our mouths meet and seal in a shivering kiss that is like no other. After the longest, skin-numbing time—

So were you and Leticia a thing before I came into the picture?

-Not a thing but not confined to the friend zone. Why?

Why do you think? Don't want to be the other woman.

-You're not.

Unburdened, Aeura releases her hold on me and begins to remove her bra and panties. I...well, I went with it and removed my boxers. It is amazing to me how those small cotton coverings could be so insulating. Sans underwear we are both flash frozen below the waist and into an embrace at the shallow end of the pool. We try to grind our way out of the discomfort. It works. Aeura, breathless, whispers.

You know a better place for us?

-I do.

And I do. The sun is at its zenith. Early afternoon, it is as warm as it will get. We climb out of the pool naked. Steam rises from our quaking bodies. It is an invitation to cling together again. And kiss, yes kiss. I have never been in this position before with a girl.

Aeura has never been with a boy. She kisses my neck and ear. I have the password of the digital lock for Mrs. Ziegler's front unit. It is furnished and there is a bed—a very big bed. We drape our dry outer garments around us, and I take Aeura's hand to lead her off—when I hear him.

Gilly, you back there?

It's Duke letting himself in through the front gate. He sees us.

I figured you might be here. Whoa! Sorry to interrupt. Celebrating the good news?

We had not heard anything and cover up as best we can. An exuberant Duke lays it out for us without showing the least bit of embarrassment about his untimely interruption. Hyung is being held at the Tombs in New York City on murder conspiracy charges.

Orange jumpsuit and all.

-I doubt his twin spawn will post that on IG.

Aeura cracks up with relish. Duke has more. Leticia and VJ got the TikTok and voicemail to the FBI and the U.S. Marshals Service. With that evidence for starters, the district attorney that AJ spoke to thinks the murder charges will stick against them.

When I say "them," this could move up the food chain to real big fish. You and your friends are kind of a big deal in town, and it's not even one o'clock.

My dad hugs me though I am still wet. He holds me like he never does. His voice cracks.

Your mother would be so proud of you, Guillermo. Me too. Sky's the limit, son. "Adversity doesn't make character…"

-It reveals it?

Aeura surprises Duke with that. He takes it as permission.

Nice! You know John Wooden. G.O.A.T. of coaches, Wizard of Westwood, never made more than $50K. You gotta love his Pyramid of Success. Me, I went pyramid scheme—my bad, gotta own it…

Duke goes on and on and kills the mood, but I know that he loves me.

one year later

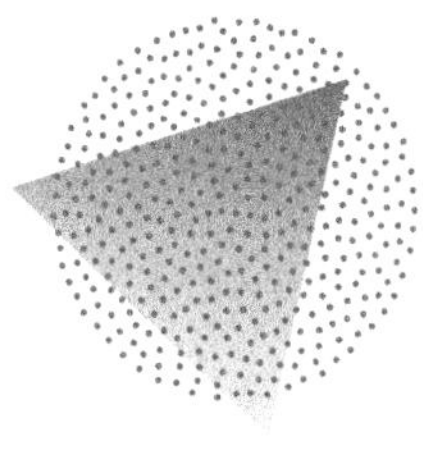

Aeura and i only had a few real opportunities after that afternoon at Mrs. ziegler's pool. I wish I could say it was magic. The next time we tried to do it, it was awkward. Aeura was sick, and I was stressed with the media attention. It all felt stilted so she balked. The other times ended up the same way for one reason or another. I can't talk about it. Her friendship was more important to me, and I didn't buck. Like Bukowski said, the days ran away like horses, so many changes and responsibilities—including our trial depositions.

The prosecutor made good use of my original recording. Replaying it over and over brought it all back vividly—the good, the bad, and the sad. After the ordeal, by the fall, individual plans got in the way. Aeura went off to visit Africa. I went to college—first in our family, not counting my overeducated Chilean cousin Nacho who always has my back. I choose UC Riverside with a full-ride scholarship. Not sure of my major yet. No hurry. I've been energized soaking in all the solid teaching—realizing, too, that I can handle it. It's been a revelation, living away from home, with the bonus of no pools to clean, though I did promise Duke I'd help him out over the break.

Okay, you should know, Leticia and VJ became an item. Iron sharpens iron. I couldn't be happier for them. Their fams are super happy too. Leticia went to UC Berkeley; he went to neighboring rival Stanford. Their future together could be "bigger than hamburger," as Duke would say. We hadn't all been together since the trials. Hyung's four-count murder conspiracy guilty verdict is under appeal. It probably will be for years, but his bail was denied, so suck on that behind bars. Boylan and Hartunian made deals. The detective got ten to twenty years, and the monster Hartunian got life. Fern's dad Phil cooperated, too, and got six months' home detention. Tomoko Kim was given community service, which seemed worse than she deserved. She lost the love of her daughter. That was her real punishment. Best of all, Owen—the Book Soup clerk—Christina, and Sidney and Delores Kim got justice.

Heading into holiday break, I was thrilled to get Fern's invitation for a weekend reunion of our Fab Five at her dad's La

Quinta desert estate. He wasn't using the estate and it was her birthday, to boot. Fern was graduating early and turning eighteen. Everyone RSVP'd to the evite.

La Quinta is southeast of Palm Springs in the Coachella Valley and is a unique desert landscape surrounded by majestic mountains on three sides. A last-century celebrity hideaway, it's always had a certain mystique. I'd been at nearby Coachella, the music festival, more than once, and this was a great excuse to return to the valley. The day had cooled down, and in the twilight it felt special here—hushed, hallowed. After identifying myself, I was welcomed by the gate guard for The Tradition, a private community, where a fixer-upper property starts at $5 million. Fern's invite to me said to arrive for the weekend fun by 7 p.m. on Friday. It was after eight o'clock when I found the address of the mid-century modern mansion. Fern answered the door. She was even more stunning than I remembered. And she was dressed for bed. WTF?!

Sorry I'm late. Where is everyone?

-Everyone else is due tomorrow.

What about the birthday party?

-Gilly, you're the party.

Fire. The kiss she planted on my ambushed lips took me into the house and beyond.

13.

rigHt Now

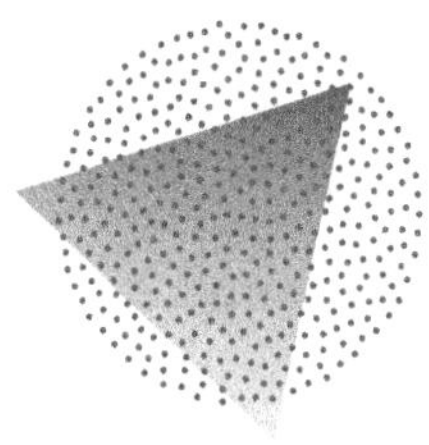

 sunken down in the swirling bubbles of the Fifer desert estate's massive flagstone spa. Above us, stars twinkle with approval in a burgeoning celestial blanket. The desert air is ripe from a recent rain, with the scent of sage and lavender, orange, and creosote. We close our eyes and identify the smells. The Jacuzzi jets are too loud, but we don't need to talk. It is Saturday night in La Quinta. I am with people I love—VJ, Leticia, Aeura, Fern. We are baked from the 103-degree water and from the Nigerian pot Aeura has snuck back into the country.

Who smuggles weed to California?

-VJ, Aeura is a disruptor and needs to show disdain for the establishment.

--Thank you, Leticia.

That is not all Aeura brought back. She has a beautiful, ebony-skinned Nigerian girlfriend who is fitting right in. One by one we step out of the whirlpooling water and into puffy white robes laid out for us by Fern's maid. Aeura is next to me. It's awkward. She leans in.

Have you been reading my travel blog?

-Oh yes. Next level. As a student I live through your adventures.

Do you like Okah? Means "princess" in Nigerian.

-She…suits you.

She will never have what we have.

Aeura softly whispers that, her breath in my ear. I am stunned and move off to grab bottled water from the outdoor kitchen. Aeura follows to explain we are like the lovers in Keats's Grecian urn poem or Lorca's under the blood moon. A pair in endless desire, who never consummate.

It's pure, Gilly. We will always have us.

Somehow, I get it.

We are all sitting in a circle around the firepit, and Fern cuddles close. I am recharged in her loving arms. She is all that I could ever imagine and all I never wanted. From a distance she is the stereotypical Beverly Hills brat. Only I know better. I know her heart and more. I know her soul. Everyone— including Okah—grins at us. Do they know that I arrived the night before and...? Of course they know. How?

We each got a call from Dr. Guttenberg last week to see if it would be all right.

-What!? VJ, you're serious?

--Availability is the best ability.

---My therapist said I had to make sure it was cool with everyone.

-Very on brand, Fern.

Everyone roars. The joke is on me and it is a sweet one. I pull Fern in closer and thank her for being so considerate.

Of course, you could have cleared it with me first.

-And miss seeing your face when I opened the door in black La Perla lace?

All agree she has a point. We are three couples now, friends, *camaradas de guerra*, and I wish this night could last forever. It is lit. More snuggling, more kisses abound in the chilly air. We are toasted by the blazing stone firepit. Okah, Aeura's gal pal, has a guitar out. In her clipped English accent, she takes requests.

All right. I got one. Classic rock. You know "Love the One You're With?"

-Seems appropriate.

--Stephen Stills. Righto.

Damn if Okah doesn't go right into the hard-strumming intro. It's a Duke favorite and a personal mantra of his. "*Love the one you're with.*" Okah has a haunting voice and can really play. Aeura accepts compliments for her.

She's good.

-We're all good.

Fern declares it. Everyone cheers. We sing along to the chorus and feel it in our bones, our oh-so-lucky bones.

"Love the one you're with…"

Am I becoming my father? Impossible. There's only one Duke. But I will always be (humble brag) the pool guy's kid.

The song ends, and it's all about the silence drifting over us. The firepit's flames dance before our eyes and animate the satisfied smiles on our faces. We are clustered together, swaying to something unheard but clear. No one photographs the moment for a later post. It feels too intimate to share. We are friends held together with one love.

Leticia, forever inquisitive, needs more.

Where will we all be one year from now?

-Only one way to find out.

--We meet here again.

---Same time, next year.

----Deal.

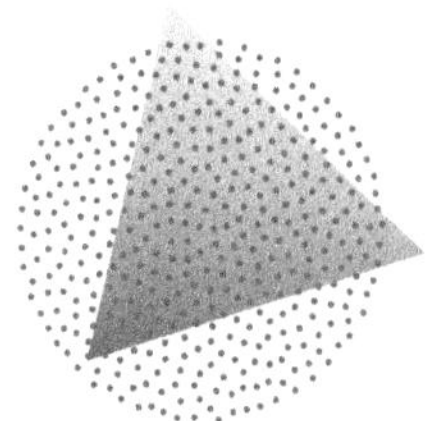

acknowledgments

I am very grateful for the input of my early readers:

dee

Mary bee

candace falk

david gerson

carol adkins

Lisa enriquez

virginia underwood

And thanks to those who frequented the novel's YouTube playlist and Facebook page, enjoying the work in progress and encouraging me through it. Plus a special shout-out to my friend in Serbia, Vladimir Lakic, and his alter ego Radoslav Celnik.

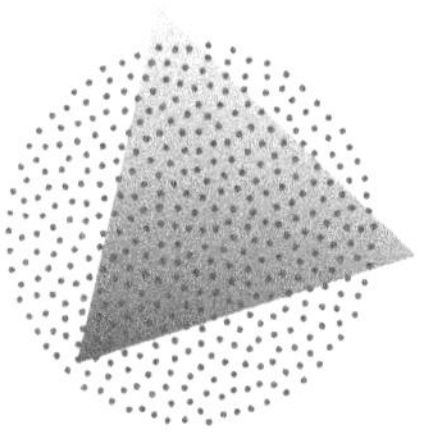

about the author

before moving to Los Angeles, Larry Mollin was a playwright and the artistic director of Homemade Theatre, a seminal performance group of the 1970s in Toronto, Canada. Transitioning to Hollywood, he wrote and produced prime time TV for over 30 years, beginning with *CHiPs*. He is best known for his work on *Beverly Hills, 90210*, for which he wrote and produced 128 hours from 1993–1998—the zenith of the show's success. Mollin returned to the theater world in 2012 with a 1960s-themed trilogy of plays produced in New York City, London, and Martha's Vineyard.

Turning to long form, he created the *Max Dean Adventures*, a trio of novels about an aging detective with a rock-and-roll background. Mollin is also a published poet and songwriter, as well as the cohost of the internationally popular podcast *Beverly Hills 90210 Show*.

Now, with *The Pool Guy's Kid*, a novel, Mollin is back in the young adult world of Beverly Hills, with a voice as fresh and witty as ever.